For more than forty years,
Yearling has been the leading name
in classic and award-winning literature
for young readers.

Yearling books feature children's
favorite authors and characters,
providing dynamic stories of adventure,
humor, history, mystery, and fantasy.

Trust Yearling paperbacks to entertain,
inspire, and promote the love of reading
in all children.

OTHER YEARLING BOOKS YOU WILL ENJOY

ON MY HONOR, *Marion Dane Bauer*

AN EARLY WINTER, *Marion Dane Bauer*

CHILD OF THE WOLVES, *Elizabeth Hall*

BIG RED, *Jim Kjelgaard*

IRISH RED, *Jim Kjelgaard*

BABE THE GALLANT PIG, *Dick King-Smith*

HARRIET'S HARE, *Dick King-Smith*

TITUS RULES!, *Dick King-Smith*

TADPOLE, *Ruth White*

OVER THE RIVER, *Sharelle Byars Moranville*

Runt

MARION DANE BAUER

A YEARLING BOOK

Published by Yearling, an imprint of Random House Children's Books
a division of Random House, Inc., New York

Visit us on the Web! www.randomhouse.com/kids

Educators and librarians, for a variety of teaching tools, visit us at
www.randomhouse.com/teachers

ISBN: 0-440-41978-6

Reprinted by arrangement with Clarion Books

Printed in the United States of America

September 2004

20 19 18 17 16 15

OPM

For my dear friends and fellow faculty
at the Vermont College Master of Fine Arts
in Writing for Children and Young Adults
program, and for the students who have
passed through my heart

——————

MY APPRECIATION TO JAMES CROSS GIBLIN,
MY EDITOR OF NEARLY THIRTY YEARS.
YOU HAVE NEVER FAILED ME.

1

Spring comes late to the forests of northern Minnesota. Geese soar in from the south, only to stand flat-footed on frozen lakes, complaining loudly to one another. Bears, groggy and cross, emerge to a world still cloaked in snow. Deer search in vain for tender shoots. Yet the wolf pups pushing their way into the world found their den warm and dry and welcoming.

Their silver mother greeted them, one by one, drying wet fur with her tongue and massaging breath into each tiny body. And though their eyes were sealed, their ears folded tightly against their heads, she could guess already what place each would take in the pack.

"Leader" she named the first brown pup, a vigorous male. The second, a female, she called "Sniffer." And she gave Sniffer's twitching nose an extra lick. Another female arrived, with spindly legs already in motion. "Runner," Silver said. "You will be swift and sure-footed, and the pack will need you." Then she drew the pup toward her nurturing body. The fourth emerged with his brow furrowed. "Thinker," his mother said fondly, licking his forehead smooth. "You will always be watching and planning, won't you?"

The den, dug into a hill above a frozen lake, angled downward from the entrance for six feet, then made a ninety-degree turn and rose for another six feet to the birthing room. The pups' father, King, a large black wolf with a white star on his chest, had been lying at the turn of the narrow tunnel, listening, waiting. As each pup emerged, his tail wagged fiercely. When the fourth pup had settled at the mother's side, King backed rapidly toward the surface.

"Four pups," he told the others waiting there. "Four healthy pups. Each one of them big and strong!" Then he danced, leaping and whirling for the joy of the new life that had come to the pack.

Helper, a young tan male born to these same parents the year before, danced, too. His silver sister, Hunter, joined them. "How fine to have pups!" they sang. How fine, too, no longer to be the youngest, the least in the pack!

Bider, a mature male, pure white, came forward. "What good news, King," he said, lowering his body and reaching up to nudge his leader's chin.

A few moments later, however, when King and the two yearlings lifted their heads to sing the new pups' praise, Bider looked on in silence. Once he, too, had been king. He'd had his own pack, his own pups to sing for. But that was before he had been deposed and driven out to hunt alone in the darkest part of winter. Now he waited, biding his time . . . and another king's pups were not what he was waiting for. He turned from the celebration.

The howl finished, King crawled once more into the den to check on his new family. Leader, Sniffer, Runner, Thinker. What splendid pups!

This time, though, he stopped, puzzled,

halfway between the entrance and the birthing room. What was that new smell? He strained to see in the deep dark of the den. The eyes of a wolf gather in even the faintest rays of light, so he could just make out the four brown furry bundles lined up along their mother's belly. They were nursing vigorously, intent on their first meal. King's tail went into motion at the very sight of them.

But Silver was busy with something more. A pup? Was she washing another pup? Yes. This one black like his father, black with a minute white star on his chest.

King's own chest swelled at the sight, and he inched forward eagerly. A look-alike son! What name would his mate choose for this son who wore his black fur and white star?

But Silver offered no name. She only went on licking.

King scooted forward further to check his son himself. He sniffed the new pup from nose to tail, tail to nose again, then drew back slowly.

Something was wrong. The black pup was small. Much too small. And he was not yet breathing.

"Runt!" The name exploded from King. "This one's a runt."

The world beyond the den was a good one, but it was hard. Only the strongest, the best, the most intelligent and competent survived in it. And sometimes not even they. Two of the pups in the last litter had died before they ever emerged from the den. Their mother had taken them, one at a time, off into the forest to bury them. Would she be doing the same again?

At last, under Silver's persistent tongue, the black pup took a breath. Then another. Air filled his tiny lungs, just as it did his brothers' and sisters', and his mother drew him gently toward her belly to begin to nurse.

Only then did Silver acknowledge her mate and the name that had sprung unbidden from his lips. "He may be Runt for now," she said, laying her chin across this latest arrival, "but who knows what gift he may bring to the pack?"

"Who knows?" King repeated softly, though wasn't the pup's mother supposed to know? She always had before. "Maybe," he added, "you have a better name."

Silver was silent for a long time. "No," she said at last, "I know no other. Not yet."

Which only confirmed King's fears. His son was marked for death.

The pups' father looked long and hard at his five offspring, especially at this last, the one whose black fur and white star filled him with such love. Then, tail wagging more slowly this time, he backed toward the surface to carry this further news to the pack.

Leader, Sniffer, Runner, Thinker. Four fine pups.

And Runt. Now there was Runt.

2

For the next few weeks Runt and his brothers and sisters emerged slowly into a world of scent and sight and sound. Their eyes opened. Stiletto teeth popped through pink gums. They drank their mother's warm milk and snuggled against her side to sleep, then woke to nurse and drifted into sleep again. Silver rarely left them except to get water, and when she did, she was always back almost before the befuddled pups had recognized her absence.

Gradually, they came to be aware of the great black wolf who came often into the den. He brought with him the rich scent of the meat he carried in his mouth for their mother or coughed up for her from his belly. But the pups had no interest in meat yet.

Gradually, too, as they crawled over the

pile of fuzzy bodies to reach milk and warmth and the comforting caress of their mother's tongue, they began to notice one another. They went from crawling to wobbling along on uncertain legs. To pouncing. To clumsy tussles.

And they grew. Their bellies constantly round and tight with milk, they doubled or tripled their weight in a week, tripled it again in three weeks. Runt grew, too, of course, but he remained the smallest, much smaller even than his two sisters. When the game was wrestling, he ended up on the bottom of the heap. When two competed for the same teat, he was the one pushed aside.

Still, he accepted his inferior size without question, as infants will. He accepted his name, too. His mother spoke it so softly, with such musical tones. "Runt. Sweet Runt. My dear little Runt." So when the day finally came for Silver to call the pups from the familiar darkness of the den, he followed without the slightest concern about what the world might hold for such a pup as he.

The last to stumble into the dazzle of a

spring morning, he paused in the mouth of the den, blinking. All around him, his brothers and sisters tumbled, emitting small, inarticulate yelps of pleasure. Only Runt stood silent, overwhelmed by the wonders spread before him.

"What is that, Mother?" he asked at last. "And that, and that?"

"That is the sky," she told him of the soft-looking blue roof above their heads. And the radiant ball that floated in it, so brilliant he had to turn his face away, was the sun. The sweet-smelling stuff riffling in the breeze in every direction was called grass, and that other sky, stretched out at the bottom of the hill below the den, was a lake.

Beyond the lake and at the edges of the grassy clearing spreading away from their den on every side, a wall of darker green rose. "Trees," Silver explained. The trees held up the sky, floated upside down in the sky lake, and whispered to one another as the wind stirred among them. *The pups are here,* Runt thought he heard them say. *See! The new wolf pups are here.*

And overlooking it all reigned the great

black wolf whom Runt had come to know as his father. King lay on a slab of rock above the mouth of the den. His golden gaze took in each of his pups in turn. *You are mine,* those eyes said. *Never forget that you are mine.*

Runt's entire body warmed with pleasure. How could he ever forget? How could he be anything but grateful for the gift of his father's world?

He had long understood that his father came and went from a place beyond the warm den he and his littermates shared with their mother. But he had never imagined King's world to be anything more than another den, perhaps deeper and darker than the one he knew. He hadn't guessed that it contained other wolves, either.

Two yearlings, a tan male and a silver female, approached the pups.

"I am your brother, Helper," said the male, bowing with front legs outstretched.

"Your sister, Hunter," the female announced.

Then they danced around the pups. "Leader, Runner, Sniffer, Thinker, Runt," they sang. "Welcome. Welcome to our world."

"Leader, Runner, Sniffer, Thinker, Runt!" called a low voice from the surrounding forest.

"The trees!" Runt cried. "They welcome us, too!"

Hunter laughed.

"That welcome comes from our friend Owl," Helper explained gently. "He often answers our songs."

"Friend Owl," Runt repeated, looking fondly at his clever brother.

A glossy black creature came floating down from the sky and landed in the midst of the pups.

"Are you Owl?" Runt asked, suddenly shy beneath the bird's bright-eyed gaze.

"Of course not," the creature replied, fluffing his feathers. "I am Raven. And who might you be?" He side-hopped a step or two, moving closer.

There wasn't much Runt knew in this unfamiliar world, but he was certain of his name. Nonetheless, his tongue seemed to freeze under this stranger's intense scrutiny.

Raven strutted around the speechless pup, examining him from every side. "You are small, aren't you?" he said at last. "Smaller than all the rest. But still"—he tipped his head to one side, considering—"small can be brave . . . fierce. Why, I've seen a pair of wrens chase a marauding crow the length of the sky. And the small red squirrel often puts the larger gray to shame."

Brave? Fierce? Runt hardly knew the meaning of the words. He liked their sound, though.

Raven stopped directly in front of Runt. "Surely, though, even a scrap of a pup like you has a name."

Runt ducked his head shyly. Perhaps Mother would answer this inquisitive bird . . . or his father, who watched them all with such observing eyes. But neither of them did.

Finally, growing impatient, Raven spread his wings, lifted off the ground, and landed on the slab of rock next to King. "You seem to have sired a pup who doesn't know his own name," he announced, cocking his head toward Runt.

King lay with his chin on his paws. He gazed at Runt but still made no reply.

"The good-looking black fellow," Raven prompted, as though King might not know which pup he meant. "The one who takes after me."

The great wolf's head came up sharply. "After *me*, Raven."

"After you?" Raven acted surprised. "How could that be? He has such intelligent eyes. And his feathers . . . they're so black and glossy."

"Fur!" King growled. "My son has fur!"

My son. Runt liked those words, too . . . even better than *brave* and *fierce*.

"Perhaps you call him Star," Raven persisted. "Since he bears your white star. Or Prince? That would be a good name for a pup who wears the king's black coat."

The silence that greeted each of Raven's suggestions seemed to give weight to the surrounding air. Even the two yearlings stared off across the lake as though there were suddenly something of great interest passing on the opposite shore.

At last, since it was clear no one else was going to answer, Runt found his own voice. "My name is Runt," he called to Raven. "They call me Runt."

"Runt?" Raven repeated. *"Runt?"* He

shook his head as though to rid himself of the sound of the name.

"Ruuuuuunnnt?" came an echo from the lake, rising and falling in laughter, though Runt had no idea who had spoken.

"That's right." A large white wolf Runt hadn't noticed before stepped into the discussion. "His name is Runt, and Loon is right to laugh." He gave Silver a bump with his shoulder. "Too bad you didn't have these pups with me," he said low, under his breath, though not so low as to keep the rest from hearing. "Then there would be no runts."

There would be no runts? Runt could barely breathe. What did the white wolf mean? That the pack would be better off without him? Runt looked once more to King to defend him. Surely, his father would stand and say it again. . . . "My son!"

And, in fact, King was rising. He stepped down off his rock and moved toward the group gathered around Runt. He walked tall on his legs, his head high, his ears pricked. But when he came close, he didn't so much as glance at Runt. He didn't defend him, either. He only lifted his tail a little higher and growled low, under his breath, "Leave her alone, Bider."

For an instant the entire forest seemed to stop breathing. Then, as suddenly as the challenge had begun, it was over. Bider lowered his head, folded his ears back, smiled ingratiatingly. "Of course, King," he whined. "I meant no harm. You know I live to please you."

"Live to please me!" King scoffed. "Don't think I don't know. You are biding your time. That's all. You live to take over my pack."

Everyone watched, waited to see what Bider would do next, but the white wolf only dropped his head lower and slunk away, his tail curved under to tuck tightly against his belly. King stood for a long moment, the fur along his spine bristling, then turned and stalked back to his place on the rock.

Silver broke the heavy silence that followed. "Come," she said softly. "We'll go inside. You've all had enough excitement for today." And nudging each pup with her muzzle, she herded them back toward the warmth and safety of the den.

Runt followed his brothers and sisters, but he kept looking over his shoulder. What had happened out there? He wasn't sure.

"Who is he, Mother?" he asked when Silver had stretched herself out in the nest at the end of the tunnel. "Who is the white wolf?"

"He is a good hunter," she said. "We've all eaten better since Bider joined us. That's all that matters."

Was it all that mattered? Runt wasn't sure. But he let the subject drop. Instead, he asked, "Is it true, what Raven said about my eyes, my feathers?"

"Fur," his mother corrected patiently. "You have fur. And Raven always has too much to say. Gossip. An opinion on every subject."

"But he said my eyes are intelligent," Runt persisted. "My feathers—my *fur*—is glossy."

Silver didn't answer. The other pups had all settled to nurse, and she began washing Leader's face.

"Mother?" Runt pleaded.

She sighed. "Raven loves nothing better than to tease and annoy your father. The two of them make a game of it. Still . . . he has been known to be wise."

Runt wanted more, but his mother was clearly not entertaining further questions. So he sighed, too, and found a place among his brothers and sisters to take his meal.

The others filled their bellies quickly and, exhausted by their excursion, soon drifted into sleep. Only Runt lay awake, reliving it all. It wasn't just Raven's praise that filled him with such awe. It was everything he had seen, smelled, touched. He could hardly bear to let the memory of it slip away, even for the length of a nap.

Would they leave the den again? Would all he had just seen be waiting for them once more if they did?

The world was so much larger, brighter, more colorful and exciting than he had dreamed! Before this morning's excursion he hadn't even known he had an older brother and sister. Or that a white wolf called Bider was part of their pack.

He hadn't known the soft blue sky or the scent of sunshine on the warming earth or that there were other creatures in the world besides wolves, either.

Or that his father was in charge of it all.

King had called him *son.* "My son," he had said.

Could anything else matter?

The small black pup closed his eyes and slept.

3

The pups made the excursion to the mouth of the den the next day and the day after that. Soon they spent most of their time out of doors, retreating to the den only at night or if their mother gave warning.

Each time the pups emerged into the day, Runt was last in line, but his enthusiasm for the world he found there never waned. When swift-footed Rabbit hopped out of her burrow, Runt raced after her. That he never came close to catching her didn't discourage him at all. Daily he chased Squirrel up a tree, then barked at him in a high, excited voice. "Come down, Squirrel. I dare you to come down!" Squirrel scolded and swore and twitched his tail in irritation. They both knew that Runt was about as likely to catch him as he was the wind, but that knowledge didn't stop them from playing the game.

Runt's zeal was far larger than his small frame and often sent him stumbling over his paws or tripping over an exposed root. Or it let him discover that the mudslide created by Otter in the lake bank was slippery, that the lake itself was cold and wet.

"Please take care," his mother sighed, licking him dry.

"Look before you leap," Helper warned, untangling him from a stand of prickly raspberry bushes.

"Stupid pup," Bider muttered, not helping at all.

Even Thinker scolded him sometimes. "Think," he warned again and again. "You've got to stop to think."

And Runt did think, of course, though usually only after he found himself in difficulty. Then he thought that if he were only a little bigger, staying out of trouble would be much easier.

Being small never kept him out of the fray, though. He and his brothers and sisters leapt at one another, strengthening muscles, improving hunting skills, jockeying for place and position in the pack. Whatever the prize might be, however, it never fell to Runt.

"Keep trying," Hunter said. "It's good practice."

"You're growing stronger every day," Helper told him.

"You're growing bigger, too," his mother often said.

But Bider, when he was near, sneered at the others' encouragement. "Bigger than what?" he would say. "A mouse? A sparrow?" For there was no question. Runt remained the smallest, the weakest, the least apt in the litter, a fact he didn't need Bider to point out.

And Runt knew that his father knew it, too. King never said anything, either to criticize or encourage. He only watched. He watched when Runt lost a game of tug of war to Runner over a bone, when Leader slapped Runt to the ground and held him there, when Silver stood to nurse the pups and Runt was the only one who couldn't reach. And always King's golden eyes seemed to ask the same question: *Can you do it? Will you survive?*

I can! Runt wanted to cry. *I can. I can.* And to prove himself, he'd go spinning after his tail until he tumbled into a dizzy heap, or he'd snap at a bumblebee and get his nose stung.

King would turn away.

Sometimes the pups took on one another's names. One morning Runner jumped on Leader and knocked him to the ground, rolling him onto his back until he squealed with indignation. For the rest of that day Runner became Leader and the first Leader was without a name. That evening, though, Leader jumped Runner from behind, flipped her over and held her down, sharp baby teeth to her throat, and their first roles were restored.

Once, when Sniffer was busy investigating a snail, Thinker noticed a stench in the air that none of the pups could name. He reported it to their father.

"It's *them*," King said darkly. "Humans." And though none of the pups knew what *humans* might be, they all crouched low in their skins and shivered.

Still, Thinker proudly took the name of Sniffer for the rest of the day.

The next day Sniffer sorted out the rich smell of a deer hidden in the trees on the other side of the lake and sent the hunters off in pursuit. The buck was strong and healthy and escaped easily, but Sniffer had her name back, nonetheless.

Runt, however, remained Runt. None of the other pups ever tried to steal *his* name.

Leader, Runner, Sniffer, Thinker. These were gifts to bring to the pack. But being a runt was no gift.

Runt refused to worry, though. He would find his gift one day. He knew he would. And with it would come a new name.

4

"It's time!" King called to the hunters.

The pack circled around the black wolf. Silver and Bider and the two yearlings sniffed his face, touched his muzzle, raised their voices in reply. "It's time. It's time," they echoed.

King tipped his head back and began a howl. The other adults and the yearlings joined in. They sang, their voices lifting and falling, twining around one another and separating again, until five wolves sounded like ten, like twenty.

The pups hadn't yet learned how to howl, but they joined the song as they could. They bunched their faces together, lifted their small muzzles to the sky, and yipped and *kay-yied* fervently.

"It's time," King said again, and he moved

out toward the surrounding forest in an easy lope.

Helper stayed behind, as usual. Since the pups had arrived, his job in the pack was to baby-sit. But the rest of the hunters fell in behind their leader, single file. Silver, Bider, Hunter—each one stepped in the footprints of the one before, so the tracks they left were nearly those of one wolf. Their big paws splayed as they touched the earth and curled as they lifted. Their entire bodies whipped forward in an easy, bouncing rhythm. They could keep such a pace, about five miles per hour, for half a day without pausing.

Once the hunters had moved out, Helper picked up a stick in his mouth, held it up in a teasing way, then ran to the middle of the clearing. All the pups except Runt tumbled after him. Runt remained where he was, gazing after the departing hunters.

To be able to hunt was a gift. It was, perhaps, the most important gift of all. If he was going to learn to be a good hunter, he needed to begin. And without a glance toward Helper and his littermates, Runt set off after the hunters.

The small black pup followed along the edge of the lake. He followed into the hushed pines. And even when he could no longer glimpse the tip of Hunter's tail ahead, just disappearing among the trees, he continued to follow, nose down, pursuing his family's warm and familiar scent.

The first time he stopped—or even hesitated—was when a grosbeak called down to him from a tall pine. "You must be King's son," he said. "You look just like him. You're small, though. Very small."

"I'm part of the hunt," Runt replied, deciding to ignore the rude remark about his size. He studied the bird's smoky red head and breast.

"I beg to differ," the grosbeak replied. "You aren't part of the hunt at all. The hunters are far ahead."

"Where have they—" Runt started to ask, but the bird had already spread his wings and risen into undulating flight.

Runt gave his shoulder a lick to wash away the insult of the bird's sudden departure. He didn't need anyone to tell him how to locate his family, anyway. He put his nose to the pine duff again and set off once more on their trail.

The scent was growing fainter, though, and as the force that pulled him along grew less strong, Runt began making various stops and detours. First he paused to listen to a chorus of peepers. Then he zigged after a swallowtail butterfly. A stream, dashing along at its own busy pace, called him for a long drink.

Runt sat back on his haunches, his muzzle dripping. Had the hunters crossed here? Snuffing along the bank, both up and down, he found no trace of their scent. Maybe it would take up again on the other side. But when Runt splashed across to the other bank, he couldn't find his pack's smell there, either. He kept moving, nonetheless. He had come too far to consider turning back.

Runt trotted, then plodded, then trotted again, though he followed nothing now, no disappearing tail, no diminishing scent. He kept going and going until finally he had no choice but to stop and admit to himself and to the watching forest that he was well and truly lost.

An enormous pileated woodpecker hammered at a nearby tree, the noise of his assault echoing through the woods. Runt sat listening, but even when the hammering stopped, he didn't attempt to ask for directions. Woodpeckers tended to be crabby fellows. Maybe it was all that pounding.

A striped chipmunk scurried past. Runt laid a swift paw on his back, holding him fast.

"Do you know where the hunters went?" he asked.

"I know where my family is," Chipmunk chittered nervously. "Nothing more."

Runt studied the bulging cheeks, the stripes, the tiny fluff of a tail.

"You're much smaller than I am," he announced finally.

"So what?" Chipmunk squeaked—rather boldly, Runt thought, for one being held down by the weight of a paw. "Now let me go. I have to carry these seeds to my family."

Obediently, Runt lifted his paw and let the little fellow scurry away. What difference did it make that Chipmunk was small? He carried seeds to his family.

Weasel emerged from beneath a tree stump.

"Have you seen the hunters?" Runt called. But the sleek brown fellow disappeared into a thicket of Juneberries without bothering to answer.

Runt was beginning to realize that following the hunters might have been a rather serious mistake. If he had stayed home, he would be napping in a comforting pile with his littermates now . . . or pouncing on patient Helper's tail . . . or simply waiting for the hunters to return with meat. He sat down in the middle of a patch of jack-in-the-pulpits and looked around. The forest was familiar but entirely strange at the same time. He was clearly far from home, and he no longer had any idea which way to turn to get back.

So he did the only thing he knew to do. He tipped his head back, drew his lips into a tight O, and began to yip and cry like any other lost pup. But after the first few yips, something unexpected happened. A howl rose on the sweet summer air. The sound startled Runt. Had it come from his own mouth? He stopped, then lifted his head and tried to yip again. Another long howl, as lost and lonely sounding as he felt, floated toward the arching sky beyond the green branches. He liked the sound, so this time he didn't stop. He just howled and howled.

"What do you want?" The voice was deep, filled with authority.

Runt looked down. A pair of large paws stood before him, slender legs, silver fur. "Mother!" he cried.

But the stern gray face towering over him was not his mother's. It was not, in fact, the face of any wolf he had ever seen before.

"Why are you in my territory?" the great wolf demanded.

Runt wanted to answer, but no further sound would come from his mouth. It was as though the remains of his voice had sailed away on the word *Mother*. He could do nothing, in fact, before this stranger but tuck his tail, lower his body to the ground, and tremble.

"Why are you here?" the wolf repeated. "I am king of this place. And you are not part of my pack."

"P-p-please," Runt stammered. "I—I'm looking for my family." He didn't dare look again into the face of the great wolf standing over him.

"Are they here?" the gray king demanded to know, the fur along his spine rising to attention.

"No," Runt admitted. "I'm the only one. And I—I seem to be lost. Just a bit."

"Just a bit," the wolf repeated, and Runt detected something in his voice that was almost a smile.

For a long moment neither of them spoke. Finally, the gray king said, "Follow me." Just that. And he turned and walked away.

Runt followed meekly. He had no idea where he was being taken, but he kept close behind the gray king, clambering over fallen trees, circling boulders, slogging through marshy patches that the other wolf stepped over or around or through without even seeming to notice. When they reached the stream Runt had crossed earlier, the king stopped and sniffed a rock standing at the edge of the water. Then he lifted his leg and left a message. *This is my territory*, the message said. *If you are a wolf, stay away!*

"I thank you," Runt murmured, stepping into the stream. "I—I'm sure my father thanks you, too."

The wolf didn't answer, only stood watching Runt cross back to his family's territory. There was, though, something in his intense gaze that reminded Runt very much of another king entirely, one who wore a black coat and carried a white star on his chest.

I will forgive your trespass, the golden eyes said, *but only because you are young and foolish . . . and small. Much too small.*

Runt ducked his head and headed away from the stream—and the watching gray king—though he still had no idea how he was going to find his family, or how he was going to find his way back to the den, for that matter.

5

Runt couldn't locate his family's scent again, so he tried to pick up his own, to follow the fragrant imprint his paws had left earlier. When he finally got hold of it, he snuffed along eagerly, only to end up at the stream once more. He had retraced his journey away from the gray wolf's realm, not the one he had made from the den.

He tried again and again, but always he found himself circling, away from the stream and back, away and back.

Finally, just when Runt was certain he would never see his family again, he picked up another scent, a very familiar one. Bider!

Runt sniffed deeply—Bider's aroma had never been so welcome—and moved forward at a lope, keeping his nose close to the trail.

He found the white wolf in a small clearing enclosed by quaking aspen trees. Obviously, the hunt had been successful. Bider's face was bloody, his belly distended. And he was so intent upon digging a hole to cache the deer haunch that lay on the ground beside him that he didn't seem to hear Runt's approach until the black pup burst in upon him, yelping with delight. Bider whirled on him with a snarl.

Runt stopped in his tracks, backing away from the fiercely exposed teeth. "It's just me, Runt. I—I'm so glad I found you."

Bider gave the pup a hard stare. "What are you doing here?" he demanded. The fur that had risen on the back of his neck began to settle again, but slowly.

"I—I," Runt stammered. "I wanted to help with the hunt. I tried to follow and got lost."

Bider snorted disdainfully and turned back to his digging.

From a respectful distance, Runt examined the deer haunch that lay on the ground. It was large and very meaty. Why was Bider burying food so far from the den? He should be taking it home to the pups, as the rest of the pack did.

Runt knew better than to ask, though. When the pack had more than they could consume in a single long feast, King cached meat, too. However, he buried it near the site of the kill, where all the hunters knew how to find it, not in some hidden place like this. King buried it and then dug it up later when food was needed at the den. Runt had a feeling, though, that this treasure would never make its way back home, except in Bider's belly.

Runt's own belly rumbled, but Bider ignored him entirely and finished digging the hole. Then he pushed the haunch into it and set to covering it. As the meat disappeared, saliva dripped from Runt's tongue.

The haunch safely buried, the white wolf finally turned and leveled a hard stare at the pup. "So you're lost," he growled.

Runt crouched, his head low, his tail tucked, and said nothing.

Bider took a step toward Runt and repeated the growl without any words this time.

Runt rolled over, exposing his throat and tender belly. *Help me,* his entire body said. *I'm only a pup. You must help me.*

Bider moved closer, straddling the black pup now. He stared down at him, his ears pricked and hackles raised.

Runt lay perfectly still, his tail tucked, his legs splayed, waiting. Was Bider going to hurt him? It wasn't possible. No wolf ever attacked another who surrendered so completely, especially a pup.

In a single swift movement, Bider lunged, his teeth grazing Runt's throat. Then as swiftly as he had started the attack, he pulled away again. Pulled away and trotted briskly out of the clearing.

Runt scrambled to his feet and hurried after Bider, assuming—hoping—that the white wolf was heading home to the den. Once Bider started moving, though, he never looked back to see if Runt was following, let alone to see if he could keep pace. The pup, already exhausted from his long trek, had to use all his strength to avoid being left behind and lost once more. As he stumbled after the disappearing flag of Bider's tail, he found himself remembering something Raven had told him.

When a king was deposed, as Bider had

once been, he was usually permitted to take a lower place in the pack. But if he'd been the kind of leader who bullied the rest of the pack, they might use the moment of his fall to drive him away. Bider must have been driven away because he was a bully.

Runt picked up his pace. Bully or not, right now Bider was the one who knew the way home, and there was little Runt could do but follow.

Only when the white wolf had almost reached the home clearing did he slow his steps, and Runt, seeing the familiar opening before him, put on a sudden spurt and caught up. The two of them entered the clearing side by side.

The rest of the pups and Helper were feasting on the meat the hunters had brought back to the den. The hunters themselves were resting, watching with pride while the others fed. When Bider and Runt came into view, King lifted his head and looked past Bider, directly to Runt. *Where have you been?* the golden eyes said. *What foolish thing have you been doing now?*

Runt cringed, knowing that he had disgraced himself. Following the hunters, getting lost, wandering into another pack's territory . . . he should have known better. But before he could even attempt an explanation, Bider spoke.

"Here is your foolish son," he said. "He ran away, but I rescued him for you."

Runt lowered his head, keeping his eyes carefully averted. Still, his father's stern gaze was like a pressure against his skin. King said nothing, but as the black pup made his way across the clearing to join his littermates at their meal, he had only one thought.

Bider had lied about his running away. That's not what he had done, and Bider knew it. He had lied about rescuing him, too. The white wolf had taken himself home, nothing more, and Runt had managed to follow.

Until this moment Runt hadn't known it was possible for a wolf to lie. What else might there be about the world that he didn't know?

Nothing that he wanted Bider to teach him, that was sure.

6

Runt didn't try to follow the hunters again. But he didn't move back into his familiar place at the bottom of the pack, either. He found a spot at the edge of the clearing beneath some fragrant balsam trees and often lay there, watching.

He watched the dragonflies skimming the surface of the lake, then swooping skyward again, their wings clacking. They were hunters, too; their prey, the droning mosquitoes.

And the redbelly snake gliding out from beneath a rotting log, and the bats crisscrossing the sky. All were hunters.

Runt watched and envied. He knew Raven had said that small could be brave and fierce, but would he ever have a chance to prove himself?

An opportunity came, finally, the day the storm blew in. The hunters were out, and Helper was in charge. He gave a short, sharp bark. "A storm is coming," he called. "Everybody in."

"A storm. A storm," the other pups echoed, tumbling over one another to reach the mouth of the den.

Runt sat at attention, observing Helper, his littermates, the roiling sky, but he didn't leave his spot at the edge of the trees to join the pell-mell rush to safety. After all, the hunters weren't running back to the den for shelter. He wouldn't, either.

When a few fat drops began to fall, Runt took little notice. He had always loved the silvery rain that worked its way through his fur to tickle his skin. He loved the wind, too, and had never entirely given up his first conviction that the trees talked when it blew.

He didn't pay much attention, either, to the odd yellowish tinge the sky had taken on or to the way the air had gone so strangely still.

When the wind rose suddenly, carrying a wall of rain toward him across the clearing,

Runt stood and, with studied dignity, moved beneath the close-standing trees. This would be shelter enough . . . surely.

Inside the forest an entirely different kind of weather prevailed. While the tops of the trees swayed and bowed in the wind's increasing force, the world at their base was calm. Even the pounding rain had gentled by the time it reached the forest floor.

Runt stood perfectly still, feeling smugly superior to his brothers and sisters huddled inside the den. He was every bit as protected and safe as they. He looked around.

Bunchberries bloomed at his feet, their tiny white flowers snug against their leaves, and the ground pine spreading across the forest floor reached for the rain as the drops trickled through. All was silvery quiet, silvery dim.

"Go home. Go home," a green frog sang from a gathering puddle, though he was clearly happy enough himself to be out in the storm.

A grouse, huddled on the limb of a tree, laughed. "*Cac-cac-cac!* What are you doing out here by yourself, foolish pup?"

Runt ignored the frog. The bird, too. He

was perfectly safe, even nicely protected. He was the king—or at least the prince—of this quiet, storm-free world. And he probably would have stood where he was through the entire storm, happily in charge of it all, if a tall pine nearby hadn't suddenly sprung into dazzling light and split in two with a bang that shook the ground beneath Runt's feet. The tree fell away from itself, crashing into other trees, cracking, crunching, grinding.

With the first sizzling bang, Runt's fur stood on end and his paws left the ground. When he landed, his legs were already moving . . . fast. A few seconds later another bolt of lightning struck a spruce, this one directly in his path, and even as he changed direction, his speed doubled.

Runt didn't know where he was headed. He was too frightened to think about going *to* anything. But every muscle in his body was trying to escape the storm that reached into his quiet world with such surging power.

Thorns caught at his fur. Long-limbed bushes slashed at his eyes. The bed of needles beneath his feet grew slippery so that he began to slip and slide and stumble over his own paws. Still he ran. Having started, he couldn't seem to stop.

The trees hissed and groaned, parting to reveal the fierce light stabbing the sky. And every few seconds the ground itself shook with the cracking thunder.

"Help me! Mother! Father! Helper! Please, help!" Runt cried. Once he even called for Bider. But no one came.

He knew, of course, that his parents and Bider and Hunter were many miles away. He knew, too, that Helper and the other pups were curled together in the dry dark of the den. He would have been glad enough himself for the den now, but he couldn't stop running long enough to sort out which direction to go to get there.

And it was no longer any consolation that the weather on the floor of the forest was quiet. The world above him sizzled and roared, and now he had proof that the sizzle and roar could reach him in an instant. He dodged trunks, slammed through underbrush, scrambled over rotting logs, crying, "Help! Help!" until suddenly, the trees parted and a clearing opened before him. At last!

Runt stopped at the edge of the trees, trembling. He had run a long distance, but he must have come full circle, because here he was, back home again. Beautiful home!

Head down, he picked his way through the slanting rain. When he reached the place where he was certain the mouth of the den should lie, he stopped. But instead of the welcoming hideaway dug into the side of the hill, an enormous structure rose before him. Trunks of trees piled on one another formed a huge enclosure. What kind of creature could live in so large a nest?

Runt knew instantly that he was in the wrong place. He knew, too, that he should return to the safety of the trees. But he couldn't seem to take another step. He stood panting, rooted to the ground, his tongue lolling out of the side of his mouth. Even when the racketing storm moved on, taking its fierce light and noise with it, even when the rain began to fall more gently, he remained utterly immobile. His terror flowed out of him like the rivulets of water that coursed over the sweet-smelling earth, only to leave him empty, humiliated. He had proved, once more, that he wasn't brave and fierce at all.

He had run, he had lost himself in confusion and panic. He had cried out for all to hear. His brothers and sisters had gone to the den as they had been told to do, and he alone had run away.

What would his father's golden gaze say when he looked at his son now?

Runt sat on the sodden ground and whimpered. Then, lifting his face to the sky, he began to howl. His howl spoke not of joy and longing, as the songs of wolves often do, but of loneliness and humiliation and sorrow. He sang of the storm that had driven him here. He sang of being the smallest, the least in the pack. He sang of the disappointment he knew would be waiting in his father's eyes when the son who ran from storms found his way back home.

Runt might have gone on singing for a long time, feeling enormously sorry for himself, had a strange creature not appeared suddenly around the corner of the giant nest.

He had never seen such a being before. It moved clumsily, standing erect on its hind legs the way Bear sometimes did. But this stranger wasn't Bear. After it came into view, it stood perfectly still, staring, and all the air grew heavy with a stench that made every hair on Runt's back rise in apprehension.

At first, Runt could do nothing more than breathe in the dark smell. But then he remembered what his father had once said when the same smell had drifted near the den. "It's *them*. Humans." The word had frizzed in Runt's blood. And every wolf in the pack had shivered.

Runt shivered now. Then he gathered himself together and turned to dash back into the forest. The human creature did not follow.

Already, though, even as Runt ran, a plan was beginning to form.

He had done it, at last. Hadn't he? Something brave and fierce and wonderful! And now he knew exactly what he would say to his father when he stood before him again.

"I walked right up to their nest and sang to the humans," he would tell the great black wolf. Then he would add, "You can call me Brave One now."

7

"Call you what?" King's voice was low, almost a growl.

"Brave One," Runt repeated, though he said it more quietly this time. With his entire family gathered around and his father peering down at him from his great height, he felt even smaller than usual. Like a pup not yet out of the den.

"I walked right up to the nest," he said again, hoping it would sound better in the second telling. "I walked right up to the nest, and I sang to—"

"Have you ever heard of such a thing?" Raven interrupted. Runt glared at the interfering bird, but Raven ignored him and went right on. "For a wolf to let himself be seen, almost touched by one of *them*. Why, I never—"

It was King who stopped the croaking chatter. When he did, Runt almost wished Raven had gone on talking instead. "A son of mine should know better." He said it quietly, but his voice was heavy with disappointment. "You should know better than to run from a storm, too. We wolves are careful. Always we are careful. But we are not afraid. Not of our own good world."

"But we're afraid of humans?" Runt didn't mean to challenge. He simply needed to understand.

"We stay away from humans," King growled. "As far away as we can. Humans mean death for wolves!" Then he turned and stalked off.

The rest of Runt's family drifted away, too, though Helper gave Runt a sympathetic glance and Silver brushed against him softly as she passed. Still, they moved away with the rest. Only Bider, who had stood listening to the whole discussion, his yellow eyes glinting in a way impossible to read, remained near.

Head down, tail tucked, Runt started toward the balsam trees at the top of the clearing again. Apparently, it was the only place he belonged.

"Coward!"

Runt stopped in his tracks. Was someone talking to him? Slowly he turned to look back. Raven had flown to his place in a tree. King lay on his slab of rock above the den. Silver had settled close by to watch over a wrestling game the other pups had begun. Hunter and Helper were down at the lake getting a drink. Only the white wolf was still close.

Bider spoke again. "Your father is a coward," he said. "He has never been near a human himself. Not once."

"Have . . . have you?" Runt asked.

Bider lifted his head. His tail came up slightly, too. "I've followed them when they come into our forest. I've watched them from the shadow of the trees. I've walked among the beasts they keep in captivity."

"And?"

"Humans are clumsy, weak creatures. They have no claws. Their teeth are dull. They can barely even run. Your father has no reason to be afraid."

"But they do smell bad," Runt offered,

knowing, even as he said it, that King must have better reason than the bad smell for his fear.

Bider tossed his head. "Your father is a coward," he said again. And he walked away.

A coward? King a coward? A cold tingle traveled along Runt's spine. Could anyone say such a thing about his father and live?

But the great black wolf had clearly been paying no attention to Bider's words. He lay placidly on his rock, flipping the tip of his tail for Leader and Sniffer to pounce on.

Runt shook himself. His father a coward? The idea was unthinkable. And yet it would not go away.

He headed for his private place at the edge of the clearing.

Still . . . if Bider was right, if it was possible that Bider could be right, did that mean that he, Runt, had been brave?

Runt curled beneath the balsam, tucked his nose beneath his tail, and thought long and hard.

8

Runt promised himself he was never going to run from a storm again. Or from anything else, for that matter. And day after day he worked to prove to his father and to the rest of the pack that he was, indeed, brave.

He was the first to leave the den, the last to return every day. He even began to challenge the other pups for the meat brought home from the hunt. Occasionally, despite his smaller size, he won out of pure determination. Once he snatched a doe's shinbone from under Hunter's nose, and when she stepped back and left the prize to him, he dragged it around all day so the rest could see. But however fearless he tried to be, his father never seemed to notice.

Then one day, wandering restlessly on the

perimeter of the clearing, he encountered a brown spiny-looking creature he had never seen before.

"Stay away from me," she muttered. "Don't you dare come near!"

"Why should I stay away?" Runt asked. He wasn't being rude. He really wanted to know. Surely, his father would take no notice of such a warning. Bider wouldn't, either.

"Because I'm dangerous," she replied. "I am the most dangerous animal in the forest."

Runt couldn't help but laugh at such a boast. He knew who the most dangerous animal in the forest was. It was the wolf, of course. Dangerous to deer. Dangerous to the enormous moose, despite their heavy antlers and fierce hooves. Even bears gave the pack a wide berth.

"Do you think you can scare me?" Runt danced on his slender legs around the creature, so low to the ground, so slow moving.

Thinker approached, too, though more cautiously. "That's Porcupine," he murmured to Runt. "I think she's best left alone."

But Runt ignored his brother. Their mother

must have made a mistake when she'd named him Thinker. He should have been called Worrier instead. He was always fretting about something.

Runt took a step closer to the short-legged animal.

Porcupine turned her back, swishing her tail in a comical fashion. The tail missed Runt's nose by inches, and he laughed again.

"I don't do battle with tails," he said. "If you want to fight, turn around and face me."

Porcupine didn't answer. She didn't turn around, either.

"Come on," Runt taunted the animal with the odd arched back and nose almost touching the ground. "Come on. Are you scared or what?"

But "what" must have been the answer, because instead of replying, she swung her tail again.

Runt jumped back. Not because he was afraid, of course—what was there to be afraid of in a tail?—but only because he wanted to prolong the game. Maybe the next time the tail came by he would grab it, show the silly creature a thing or two.

First he would capture the tail, then the whole beast. He would drag Porcupine back to the den for a small feast. Then his family could call him Provider, conqueror of the "most dangerous animal in the forest"!

"Runt," Thinker scolded, "be care—"

The tail swung once more and Thinker, so busy warning Runt that he was unprepared himself, slipped and lost his footing when he tried to move away. To Runt's surprise, his brother shrieked, a piercing scream Runt had never heard from any pup before.

When the offending tail came back, Runt lunged to grab it. But even as he tried to take hold, pain flashed through the side of his face, pain so fierce that he couldn't even cry out. A dozen stabs below his right eye and all along his jaw took his breath away.

Thinker was still screaming, but Runt could no longer consider him. He was, himself, stumbling, crying . . . trying to outrun the searing pain.

Where he was going he had no idea. He barely took note of anything before him. He could tell only that he was moving away from Thinker—or perhaps his brother was moving away from him—because the crying sounds grew more distant.

Discovering himself at the edge of the lake, Runt buried his stinging face in the cold water. But even that gave no relief. Barbs had driven themselves through his skin, into his mouth. He slapped at the long prickers, rising onto his haunches and using both paws to bat and pull at them. But that did no good. The pain, which he had thought could be no greater, only grew worse.

Runt raised his wounded muzzle to the sky he had loved since his first day out of the den and cried, "Help me. Someone please help me!" In the distance, he could hear Thinker uttering the same cry.

Helper and the other pups answered, but from far away, too. Far away and growing farther. The yearling and the other pups must have run to help Thinker.

"Always we are careful," Father had said. "But we are not afraid." But how could a pup anticipate disaster waiting in every creature's tail and not be afraid?

Foolish. King's gaze had said that, too.

Runt wanted to roll on the ground, to

smash his muzzle into the earth, to howl. But gradually he went quiet instead. Every movement, even every utterance only made the fire in his face worse, anyway. He crawled from the grassy bank and stumbled toward the wall of trees.

He was going to die. He knew it. The way the little field mouse had died when he had pounced on it, going suddenly limp and soft in his jaws. The way the deer did and the great moose the hunters brought home in their bellies. He would die and be food for maggots and mice, for weasels and skunks, perhaps even for Raven.

Once again, he had done the wrong thing. Done the wrong thing and brought his brother down with him. What right did he have to live? Runt stepped beneath the shelter of a pine tree, and the entire grove reached out to surround him.

He plodded on. Every time he came to a place where he might have collapsed, where he might have waited for death to take him, the pain kept him stumbling forward. He moved past the remains of a bear's winter nest gouged out beneath a boulder, past quaking aspen and whispering spruce. He kept going until the agony in his face had grown beyond endurance. Only when he came to the clearing did he stop at last.

The moment he reached it, he knew it was *the* clearing, the one where he had encountered the human creature. He started to turn back. Then he stopped.

Humans mean death for wolves. That's what his father had said. His father, who thought he was "foolish," "afraid."

For a time Runt stood perfectly still, trembling in the shadow of the trees. Then he stepped bravely out into the clearing, sat back on his haunches in full view of the humans' strange nest, and tipped his burning face to the sky.

"Come and get me," he sang. "I'm here. I'm ready to die."

9

When the shadow fell across Runt, he sank to the ground. It was, as he had fully expected, one of—*them*. A human.

He went utterly still. The dark odor enveloped him and the strange furless paws reached down and lifted him. His heartbeat slowed, his muscles went limp. It was the same way he reacted—the way all pups reacted—when being lifted and carried in his mother's mouth.

Even when another human appeared and the two hovered over him, gabbling incomprehensibly, he lay in the creature's arms, perfectly still, waiting. He knew that whatever was going to happen next was beyond his control.

The one who had lifted him carried him to a place near the human nest, then put him down, but continued to hold him. Runt didn't struggle. He had no strength to run even if he had been let free. The other produced a hard object and began pulling the quills, twisting and turning to get past the cruel barbs. Runt cried out once, a high, sharp yip, then let himself slip into an even deeper stillness. The pain and the relief from pain were so mixed that he hardly knew whether to tear at his captors or to lick them in gratitude. And so he did neither. He just waited for all to be over. Waited, still, to die.

When the humans had pulled the last of the barbed quills from his muzzle, they released him. Runt didn't move. He kept his eyes down, careful not to look at them directly. They were a great deal larger than he. Larger, even, than his father. Who knew what they might do if they were challenged?

He had never encountered more ungainly creatures, though. As Bider had said, they were clumsy and weak. How could they possibly make their way in the world? They didn't even have any feathers or fur to cover their ugly bodies.

The humans stroked him and set water

before him. They put down some strange kind of meat, too. Then they went away. Runt watched them go, then slowly, cautiously, looked around the clearing. He was close inside the shadow of the enormous nest, but nothing stood between him and the forest. Apparently, he was free to go.

Nonetheless, he remained where he was, perfectly still. Where would he go if he returned to the forest? Back to suffering Thinker, whose warnings he had ignored? Back to his father with this new tale?

At last, he dragged himself to his feet, examined the meat and the water the humans had left, then, without sampling either, found a dark corner behind a heavy object and curled into a tight ball.

His father was wrong about one thing, for certain. Humans did not mean death for wolves. These creatures had helped him.

Maybe, after all, this human place was where he belonged.

10

Runt woke to moonlight and to a rough tongue scouring his face.

"Mother!" He leapt to his feet.

But the beast licking him was not his mother. She was about the same size as Silver. Heavier in the body, perhaps. Not as long in the legs. Her coat was reddish gold, her eyes mild in a way Runt found disconcerting.

Everything about the creature reeked of humans.

"Who . . . who are you?" Runt stammered.

"I am Dog." She spoke softly. "They call me Goldie."

He studied Goldie's face. It was pleasant, even kindly, but somehow not especially intelligent.

"Do you know the humans who live here?" he asked, feeling strangely as though he should be the one taking care of her. "Did they help you, too?"

Her brow furrowed. "Know the humans? Of course. They are my masters."

Masters? It was a new word for Runt. A strange one.

"I *belong* to them," Goldie added, as though the word *belong* would help him to understand.

It didn't. Goldie wasn't a puppy. She was even well past being a yearling. Adult wolves honored their leaders. They honored them because the leaders were strong, skillful hunters, wise in the ways of the world, but they never *belonged* to them. They belonged only to themselves.

"But why?" Runt asked. "Why would you let them own you?"

"They feed me," Goldie replied cheerfully. "They scratch me behind the ears. They get out my leash and take me for walks."

Runt could understand the importance of being fed. The adults in his pack fed him, after all. And he loved being groomed. But being *taken* for a walk? "What is a *leash*?" he asked.

"It's a kind of rope," Goldie answered.

"They tie it to my collar . . . here. See?" Goldie scratched at a tight band around her neck that Runt hadn't noticed before. "And then they take me with them when they go out."

Runt shook his head. He couldn't seem to understand, though Goldie spoke clearly enough.

"The humans are so clumsy," he said, "so slow moving! Surely, you don't let them tie you to them!"

But Goldie seemed offended by his question. "Of course I do! They take care of me. Don't you understand?"

Runt shivered. This dog was little better than a prisoner! No animal he knew kept another captive in this way. Still, when Goldie bent to lick Runt's sore face once more, he closed his eyes, enjoying the touch of her gentle tongue.

"Where did you come from?" she asked between licks. "Who took care of you before my humans found you?"

And so Runt told about his kindly mother, his proud father, the cozy den he had been born in, his brothers and sisters there. He even told her about Bider, though he didn't mention that Bider had once called his father a coward.

"Goodness," Goldie said at last. "So many of you. Who sees that all of you are fed?"

"The hunters. They go out and find food for all the rest."

"Every day?"

"Well, no . . . they don't bring food every day. When they can make a kill, they do. When they can't . . ." The intensity of Goldie's stare stopped Runt's explanation.

"When they can't?" Goldie prompted.

"Why, of course, we wait." It seemed an odd question. When the pack had food, everyone ate. That was all. When they didn't, what else was there to do but wait for the next hunt? The hunters missed far more frequently than they scored—about three attempts out of four ended in failure. That was the way of hunting. Still, they brought food home often enough to keep the pack healthy.

"My owners give me food every day," Goldie said, and there was a note of finality in her voice, as though eating every day were very important. Perhaps the most important thing of all.

Runt glanced over at the bowl the humans

had put meat in for him and saw that it was empty. Apparently, Goldie had enjoyed the food her humans had left for him, too.

But who needed to eat every day except for a nursing baby? Was this why Goldie seemed so soft, so like a pup despite her mature years? Because she sat around waiting for someone to feed her, day after day?

Runt thought of the humans he had seen, their clumsy walk, their unprotected skin, their dull teeth. "Where do your humans hunt their food?" he asked. "How do they kill it?"

But clearly Goldie didn't know, because she only looked at him blankly.

"Haven't you ever asked them?" Runt prompted.

"Of course not," Goldie replied. "They wouldn't understand if I did."

Runt was amazed. He had noticed the humans' strange, incomprehensible gabbling, but he had thought . . . well, he didn't know what he had thought, exactly. He moved closer to Goldie, speaking distinctly, in case she was the one who might fail to understand. "Any squirrel or rabbit, any chipmunk can carry on a conversation! You can, too."

"Not with them." Goldie rose to check out Runt's bowl again. She licked it thoroughly, though it was quite clean already. "When I want food, I bump my bowl around. When I want to go out, I take them my leash . . . or scratch on the door. They understand simple things like that. But there is no point in *talking* to them."

"You mean"—Runt was amazed—"they can't talk at all!"

"Oh," Goldie paused to scratch at her collar again, "they can say a few words. But not enough to carry on a real conversation."

"What kind of words?"

"Like *sit* and *come. Fetch. Bad dog.* A few words like that."

Sit? Come? Fetch? Bad dog! "And what do you do when they say those words?" Runt's question was almost a whisper.

"I do what they tell me, of course. And then they give me treats."

Runt stood suddenly. He began backing away. "I—I've got to go." He was almost panting. "My family is waiting. I've got to go home."

Goldie didn't move. She simply sat there,

watching him with her mild brown eyes. Her look said clearly that she thought he was silly to leave but that she was much too polite to say so.

"Come with me," he said. "Come and meet my family. I'll show you life in the forest. It is good."

"Thank you." Goldie rose, and for a moment Runt thought she was going to join him. Then she shook herself and sat back on her haunches once more. "You are very kind," she added. "But I belong here. Don't you understand?"

Runt didn't understand, but even as Goldie spoke, he noticed something he hadn't before. Goldie couldn't have followed him even if she had wanted to. A long chain attached to the collar around her neck was attached also to the corner of the human nest. Runt stared, horrified. Then, not wanting to embarrass the gentle creature, he turned and hurried away.

He crossed the clearing at a trot and, without a glance back toward Goldie or her jailers, slipped into the welcoming arms of the forest.

11

When Runt reached the trees, he began to run. "I'm coming," he called to anyone who cared to listen. "I'm coming home."

A white-throated sparrow answered with its achingly pure song. Owl hooted from the top of a tall pine. Even a friend of Raven's called down in a friendly way, "Hurry, little pup. You'd better hurry."

And Runt answered each voice with his own high, keening cry.

He had a choice. No one was holding him prisoner. And his choice was to go home!

His paws danced past lady's slippers, leapt over wild strawberries, skipped by maidenhair ferns.

Home! And his family would be so glad to see him!

Had anyone else in his family ever made friends with a dog? Had anyone else actually been touched by a human and lived to tell the tale? Even Bider?

Runt loped past a doe chewing her cud. He sent a night-prowling raccoon scurrying for cover.

"Humans touched me," he sang, "and I am still here. They touched me, and I did not die."

His father would probably be glad to know that he had been wrong! Wolves didn't need to fear humans. Humans brought life, not death.

When Runt arrived home at last, he trotted out of the trees, his face lifted, his voice high. "I'm home," he yipped. "I've come home. Look at me. I'm here."

All the pack lay or sat in a tight little group, close by the mouth of the den. Only his mother lifted her head, rose, and started toward him. When she had come half the distance, though, she stopped.

"You've been with *them*," she said, her voice sharp, even accusing.

"Yes," Runt cried. "I've been with them."

And he did a little dance. "Isn't it wonderful? I've been with them, and I survived. They pulled all the quills Porcupine left in my face. And I'm fine now. Can you see?"

Helper approached, too, but he also stopped some distance away, sniffing the air with clear distaste.

The elation that had carried Runt home began to trickle away.

Others in the pack moved toward him, but none came close. Only King remained where he was, standing over something Runt couldn't see.

"They helped me," Runt repeated, more quietly.

Without another word, his mother turned away. The pups who had approached him and the two yearlings did, too. They all followed Silver.

"I met Dog," Runt called after them. "Has anybody else here ever met a dog? Her name was—"

"Hush!"

Runt looked up to see Bider standing over him.

"Hush," the white wolf said again, as

though the first command hadn't been enough. "No one here appreciates your adventure. They're too busy worrying about Thinker."

"Thinker?" And suddenly Runt remembered. The humans had helped him, but Thinker had been hit, too. In all his strange and bewildering adventure, he had forgotten about his brother.

Runt approached the group slowly. They were, indeed, gathered around Thinker. Not only did he have quills in his muzzle and the side of his face as Runt had once had, but one long quill had pierced an eye. Thinker whimpered softly. Something about the pup's low whimper was more pitiful even than his screams had been the day before.

Runt leaned over his brother. "Come with me," he whispered. "I know where you can get help."

Thinker opened his good eye, but then let it flicker closed again.

"Thinker!" Runt leaned closer. "You've got—"

King stepped up. "Where do you want to take my son?" he demanded to know.

Runt glanced up at his father, then quickly lowered his gaze. Now was his chance to tell King everything, all he had learned about humans.

"You've been with *them* again," Hunter interrupted before Runt could gather his thoughts. "You positively stink of *them!*"

"Yes," Runt admitted, "but—"

And before he could explain, before he could tell them that it was humans who had removed his quills, the circle of his family closed around his brother again, shutting him out.

"He was with *them!*" one pup murmured to another. "He was with the humans!" And they all shuddered.

Runt stood for a moment, motionless, frozen. Then he turned and plodded away.

He found Raven by the lake getting a drink of water. "Is it such a terrible thing," he asked the glossy bird, "to be helped by humans?"

Raven, the usually talkative Raven, only spread his wings and flew away.

Runt plunged into the water. He knew washing would do little to remove the stench he had carried back with him. He must stink of Dog, too. But at least bathing was something to do.

He almost wished Raven had scolded him in his usual bossy way. Or even his father. Anything would be better than this silence, the silence of his family gathered around his wounded brother.

"I should have stayed," he said, mostly to himself. "I should have stayed with Dog and with *them*."

Though when he thought of the chain that held Goldie prisoner, he couldn't help but shudder, just as the others had when they realized where he had been.

12

Thinker died slowly. Each day his whimpers grew more faint. Each day the pack grew more silent.

Bider went off by himself and came home with a fat beaver, but Thinker could not eat. He couldn't even rouse himself to go down to the lake for water.

"My son," King said, again and again. "My son. My son." But Thinker no longer responded to the sound of his father's voice.

Runt heard, though. The words went through him like another quill. When had he last heard King speak to him in such a way?

When Thinker finally took his last breath, when his chest rose and fell once, twice, three times, and then no more, the entire family gathered for a long, mournful howl.

Only Runt remained silent, though no

one seemed to notice. These days no one noticed much of anything about him except that he had been touched—contaminated—by humans.

His mother held him down with a firm paw and washed him every time she came near. Sometimes Helper did the same. But neither of them said much to him.

His father didn't speak, either, though at least his silence was familiar. What was not familiar was that King had quit watching Runt, quit taking note of his every foolish act, his every mistake. It was as though two of King's sons had died from the porcupine's blow, not one.

I am alive, Runt reminded himself. *The humans helped me, and I am alive.*

If existing on the edge of the pack could be considered living.

13

A few days after Thinker's death, the wolf family set off for a new home. It was past time for the move. Thinker's prolonged dying had kept them close to the den long after they ordinarily would have left.

The pups were old enough now that they didn't need the warmth and protection of the den, and the family required a new hunting range. They set out at a gentle lope in their usual single file, carrying nothing with them but their warm fur, their powerful, graceful bodies. King, Silver, Bider, Hunter, Helper. Followed by the pups. Leader, Runner, Sniffer . . . Runt.

No one told Runt to follow at a slight distance, but he did. No one called him to close the gap, either.

King chose a new site on a brushy hillside.

Nearby a gurgling stream dropped to another placid lake. *They're here,* the stream murmured to Runt's ears. *The wolf pups are here!*

But where is Thinker? the rippling lake asked.

"Gone," Runt answered mournfully. "Thinker is gone."

The other pups discovered a grassy indentation where they could curl together for warmth when the nights were cool. King chose the rise that gave the best overview of the surrounding area. Silver found a place near her mate. Bider settled to one side and just below them both. The two yearlings stayed close, too. Runt sought out the shade of a solitary maple at the far edge of the clearing and turned and turned, trampling the grass to make himself a solitary bed.

And so the summer progressed. The hunters went out and came back again. When they were successful, they brought food for the entire family, mostly deer, occasionally moose. When they weren't successful, everyone waited for the next hunt and hoped it would be better.

Something important had changed since

Runt's last adventure, however. The other pups played among themselves, seldom inviting Runt to join them. He couldn't tell whether they were afraid of him or disdainful. He knew only that while the humans had saved his life, they had also left their mark.

His mother, of course, remained his mother, though she continued to show her affection by giving him a good wash. Runt wondered, sometimes, if he would ever smell right to her again.

And his father? King seemed sad, abstracted. Sometimes he went off into the forest alone. What he did there, Runt couldn't guess. He never returned with food.

Helper, apparently feeling sorry for the outcast, began to spend more time with Runt. He singled him out for play, teaching him new skills. Runt accepted his brother's attentions gratefully.

A large family of Canada geese lived on the lake. When the adults molted, leaving them as flightless as their gangly young, Helper often signaled Runt to join him. Together they crept through the long grass until they were close enough to leap, sending the startled geese flapping their useless wings and braying into the lake. Helper and Runt always ended by splashing their paws in the shallows, rejoicing in their joke.

Helper taught Runt to run in step behind him, to move fluidly and silently through the grass. He even taught Runt to scent a cow moose with twin calves as much as four miles away. Still, Runt never again tried to follow when the hunters left on their search for food.

Runt fed when the others did, jumping up to bump a hunter's mouth to beg the food brought back in their bellies. He joined his littermates in games of tug of war with the bones and chunks of meat the hunters brought back, too. Once he even helped Sniffer locate the haunch of a deer King had cached near the clearing against a hungrier time. For their transgression, their father disciplined them equally with bites on the tops of their muzzles.

One day the pups discovered Skunk, their noses twitching at the compelling and disgusting smell that hung around the waddling black-and-white creature. Runt was the only one with enough sense to stay back, proving his encounter with Porcupine hadn't been entirely in vain. But it gave him little pleasure to avoid sharing his littermates' smelly fate. His good fortune seemed only to prove in another way how little he belonged.

As the summer moved on, the pups' eyes changed from blue to the deep yellow of a mature wolf's. Their down-soft puppy fur was replaced by sleeker adult coats. And, of course, they grew. Their already-long legs, their big paws and tall ears grew even faster than the rest until their body parts seemed awkwardly mismatched. Runt changed and grew with the other pups, but he remained the smallest. And he was still Runt.

"Why," he asked Helper one day, "did my mother give me such a cruel name?"

"Didn't you know?" he replied. "Our mother didn't name you. Father did."

Father! His father had named him Runt!

Raven, who had been listening in on the conversation, intruded with his own comment. "There is nothing wrong with being small. Why I've seen a pair of wrens—"

"Yes, yes, I know," Runt snapped. "They

chased a crow across the sky." And he turned
away.

Autumn approached. Sumacs blazed red, the
topmost branches of the maple tree Runt
often rested beneath burst with color. The
leaves of the aspens shivered on their slender
stems, giving out a rattle as dry as death.

Bears ate their languorous way through
the forest. Small red squirrels showered the
ground with pinecones, as many as a hun-
dred in an hour, then scurried down to gather
them up to store against the coming winter.
The reddish brown coats of the deer dulled to
bluish gray.

Some days the hunters were successful
and the pack lay in the cooling sunshine,
gorged and contented. Sometimes they
returned home with bellies still empty.

It was after several unsuccessful hunts
that Raven flew overhead. "Moose!" he called.
"Moose!" He often flew in with reports of
game nearby. When wolves eat, ravens eat, too.

The pups stopped their play. The adults
woke from their napping or half napping
states, suddenly alert.

King rose to his feet. "Where?" he asked.

"This way!" Raven croaked. "Very near." And he flew off across the stream into the forest. The wolves all stood, watching the bird's departure, their ears pricked and their noses working.

King tipped back his head and howled. Silver joined him, and the others gathered around, adding to the song. "Moose!" the song said. "There are moose waiting for us out there."

Their voices started low, then rose and rose, each on a different note, until the entire forest reverberated with their presence. Even the pups joined in . . . except for Runt. He had not howled once since he had sung his way back through the forest from the human place.

Raven flew back. "Don't sing," he scolded. "It's time for action. Let's go!"

"Come!" King called. And to Runt's amazement, this time he looked directly at the pups.

Runt's heart raced. Could his father possibly be calling the pups to join the hunt? Even him?

"Come!" King said again, and his meaning was clear. The pups were to go on their first hunt!

Runt wagged his tail and looked at Helper, who wagged his tail, too. "Now," Helper whispered, "you can use what I've taught you."

Runt intended to do exactly that. He would prove himself to Helper. He would prove himself to his mother and to Bider, too.

Especially, though, he would prove himself to the one who had named him Runt.

14

King took the lead, and the rest of the pack followed in their usual order. The adults set a steady pace, but the pups' legs had grown long enough over the summer that they were able to keep up.

The pack moved silently, crossing the stream and angling off in the direction Raven had shown them, their noses testing the air.

King was the first to pick up the scent. He stopped abruptly. "There," he told the others. "Just there. Close!"

Sniffer got it next. "There!" she echoed in a high, excited voice.

And then the rest, including Runt, could smell it, too.

They circled around King, touching his nose, wagging their tails, savoring the rich, good smell of moose. *There*, the breeze told them. *Just there!*

"Come!" King said again, and they moved out in the same unerring line.

After a short distance, King called out, "At the edge of the woods, in the long grass. Lying down."

The message passed down the line. "At the edge of the woods. In the long grass. Lying down."

"If he refuses to run," King commanded, "drop back. The ones who hold their ground are young and strong. We don't want a fight."

Again King's words passed back along the line, this time accompanied by Bider's muttering.

"We're hungry," Bider complained. "Don't tell us to give up before we've even begun."

Runt heard it all, his father's words and Bider's complaints. He didn't know which one he should listen to. He, too, was hungry. He knew that.

The wolves ran full out until the scent they pursued was overwhelming. Then, suddenly, King slowed and the pack slowed behind him. They crouched lower, moving with more deliberate steps, their heads thrust forward.

Moose! Moose! The scent sang in Runt's brain as it sang for every other wolf in the pack.

"There!" King said, and that word passed along the line, too.

"There . . . there . . . there . . . moose is there."

And then an enormous creature came crashing to his feet, rising out of the long grass where he had been lying. It was a bull moose, full grown, enormous. Would he stand? Would he fight? Would they return home with their bellies still empty and aching?

For a long moment the moose remained still, peering at the approaching pack with small, nearsighted eyes, and the wolves fanned out, forming a half circle, waiting their chance.

I know, the moose's eyes said. *I know you have come to kill me. But I won't go without a fight.*

Runt was stunned at the size of the beast. He hadn't realized anything could be so large.

And glancing at his littermates, he was certain they were as overwhelmed as he with the fellow's size, with his smell, with being part of the hunt for the first time. Sniffer trembled, even as she savored the rich scent of the beast before them. Runner and Leader danced forward, then back again, forward and back.

Even King hesitated, sizing up the beast.

Bider stepped out ahead of the rest, moving closer to their quarry. "Come on," he prodded. "Don't lose this one."

And then their chance came. The moose's courage failed, and he turned and lumbered away. The pack dashed after.

"It's an old one," Silver said, passing the word to the pups. "We have a chance."

And watching the moose run, Runt could see what his mother meant. The huge animal carried himself with a towering dignity, but his gait was stiff. He seemed to be a bit lame on the left side, too. And though he picked up speed quickly, the wolves were easily able to match him.

King and Bider jumped at the moose's rump, slashing, drawing blood in streams. Hunter and Silver ran past them. They leapt and clung to the beast's shoulders, one on each side. Helper put on a burst of speed and got in front of the great animal's head. Then he turned back. With a lunge, he leapt to take hold of the beast's leathery nose, grabbing on, swinging free with all four feet off the ground.

The moose bellowed but didn't slow his pace.

Already Runt could taste the fresh meat. He longed to take hold, too . . . anywhere. And though his heart was hammering in his chest, he pushed and pushed until he had moved past the rest of the pups and was right on the great beast's heels. Then he plunged forward, grabbing for the back of one leg.

The next thing Runt knew he was flying through the air, flying and landing, too hard. He lifted his head, struggling to pull air into his lungs again, and from that position, flat on the ground, he observed the rest of the action. The bull moose brushed one shoulder against a slender aspen, strong and straight. Silver crashed to the ground, twisting as she fell. Then the great creature passed close to a tree on the other side. Hunter's hold was jerked free, and she, too, landed unceremoniously on the ground.

Now only Helper had a hold, swinging from the beast's nose. And as the moose continued to stagger forward, he swung his huge head, hurling the yearling wolf this way and that. Helper might have been a leafy branch buffeted by the wind. With the next sweep of the bull's enormous head, the yearling's body smacked into the trunk of an oak tree. Hard. Then the moose swung his head back and drove the young wolf into an elm on the other side.

Helper dropped to the ground like a rock.

In the sudden silence that followed, the bull moose disappeared into the forest. Only Bider still pursued him.

Silver and Hunter rose from where they had fallen. Silver limped, but she led the way toward the place where Helper lay. Runt rose, too, and the pups and Hunter followed close on their mother's heels. King joined them all.

Silver sniffed Helper's face, his eyes, his ears. Then the silver wolf whimpered and stepped back. The others approached, sniffed, whimpered, one after the other. Helper did not stir. Only Runt stayed back.

King licked his son's face, just once, then turned away. "Come," he said to his family. It was an entirely different call than the one with which they had begun the hunt.

Even Silver hesitated, looking down at her fallen son, but then she whined, sniffed Helper again, and followed her mate.

Runt stood alone beside Helper's still form, frozen into place. How could his family leave . . . ?

"Come along," Hunter commanded, moving the pups forward with gentle bumps of her muzzle. "Come along."

"But . . ." Runt dropped stubbornly to the ground, glancing over his shoulder at his parents, who were now some distance away, walking with their heads down. His mother's limp looked bad. "We can't leave Helper here. He needs us!"

"Helper will never need us again," Hunter replied softly. "Now come." And she and the other pups moved off after their parents.

But Runt did not come. He laid his chin across Helper's tan chest and watched his family go. He didn't understand. If there was truly nothing they could do for his brother, then why didn't his father follow Bider and continue the hunt? Bider had been right about one thing. They were hungry. They were all hungry.

Long after the rest of his family was gone, Runt lay next to his brother's still body. The light sifting through the trees grew dim, and the bright gold of Helper's steadfastly open eye grew even dimmer, but yet Runt did not move. Flies began to settle on the golden eye, on the dark lips. They crawled into Helper's ears. A turkey vulture had come to perch on a branch overhead, then another. How quickly news traveled in the forest.

But Runt took little notice of any of it until Raven dropped out of a tree, landing near him.

Runt raised his head slowly. "Not you, too," he said. "Are you waiting for me to leave so you can feast?"

"Of course not." Raven ruffled his feathers the way he always did when he was offended. "I have some loyalty, you know."

Runt snapped at one of the endless flies

buzzing around his head, then settled his chin once more across his brother's still body. The warmth of Helper's life had slipped away.

"Did Bider bring down the moose?" Runt asked.

"Bider is still running," Raven replied. "Trying to bring down that old bull alone, even injured as he is now, is going to keep him running for a long time."

Alone. The pack should be with him. Why had his father given up so easily? Was it true that he was afraid? Runt wanted to ask Raven, but he didn't. He knew that Raven, for all of his constant quibbling with King, would only defend his father.

In the distance, voices rose. Runt lifted his head. His family had begun a howl, a song of Helper. His life. His death.

Runt pointed his nose at the fading sky, ready to join the song, but no sound came from his throat. He lowered his head, laying it across his brother's body again. After all, no one had asked him to join them.

"Aren't you going home?" Raven asked. "Or are you going on with Bider?"

Runt considered. Those were the choices. Go home, where he had no gift to give—not even his voice—or join Bider on an impossible quest.

Surely, no one missed him at home. And the flight he had taken off the old moose's leg had taught him how little use he would be in this hunt.

He closed his eyes.

When he opened them again, Raven was gone. The light was gone from the forest, too. Helper's body was stiff. The vultures sat like stones in the tree just above them, waiting. No doubt other forest creatures waited, too. Not to mention the hordes of insects and the worms that had already begun silently to feast on the young wolf's body.

The gift of Helper's life was returning to the forest. Back to them all. As young as he was, Runt understood that. He understood, too, that there was nothing more he could do here.

He rose and began plodding deeper into the forest, following the trail left by the wounded moose. Whether he could be any help in the hunt or not, at least he would find Bider.

15

Despite the hours that had passed, the trail was easy to locate. The enormous moose had crushed bushes, wounded trees, dripped blood. And so Runt put his nose to the ground and followed. His shoulder was sore from the kick he had received and had stiffened during the time he had been lying with Helper, but he ignored the pain and concentrated only on the trail.

He would help Bider. He would help Bider bring down the moose. And when they arrived home to the pack, their faces bloody, their bellies full, dragging a chunk of meat between them for the rest to feast on, they would both be heroes. Even he, Runt, would be a hero.

As Runt loped along, he remembered the sensation of sailing through the air, thrust by the moose's kick. He was lucky, he knew, that the kick had only thrown him, not crushed his skull or broken other bones. But even remembering this, he stayed on the trail. He needed food. They all needed food. And with food would come a place in his family.

Runt finally found Bider lying in a patch of morning sunlight by a small stream. The moose was nowhere in sight.

Runt approached slowly. "I came to help," he said.

"Help?" Bider snorted. "Some help you would be. It's your father I need. Your father and Hunter and Helper and—"

"Helper is dead," Runt interrupted.

"Silver," Bider finished, as though Runt hadn't spoken. "Silver is a fine hunter. I would be glad to have her at my side."

Runt sat down next to the white wolf, just sat there and watched the stream burble past.

"We could have taken that moose, you know," Bider said at last. "If we'd only stayed together, we could have run him to the ground and taken him. Our bellies would all be full by now."

"I know," Runt said.

"He's a coward," Bider added.

"Who?" Runt asked. But of course, he knew that, too.

"Whooo?" a voice repeated from a spruce tree near by. "Whooo?" Owl with his endless, foolish questions.

In any case, Bider didn't bother to answer either of them.

When Bider and Runt arrived back at their new site, the pack had scattered over the hillside. There was very little activity. Even the pups lay still, not pouncing on one another or wrestling or investigating whatever moved in the grass. King was in his usual spot. As Bider and Runt stepped into the clearing, King's gaze slid across Runt and settled on the white wolf. But what those amber eyes saw, Runt could not even guess. Did his father know that he had followed Bider, ready to help him take the wounded moose for the family?

Silver lifted her head to acknowledge Runt's return, but she didn't rise to welcome him. Not even to give him another wash.

Runt told himself he didn't mind. He certainly didn't need bathing. Still, something inside him ached in a much deeper way than the sore muscles left by the moose's kick.

Bider stalked to the edge of the clearing and threw himself down. He lay there briefly, then rose to choose another spot. Then another. Finally, he marched over to King.

"You can't expect me to do it all alone," he said.

King lifted his head. "Do what alone, Bider?"

"Feed this family."

"No," King replied solemnly. "I can't expect you to do it all alone." And then he settled his chin on his paws and closed his eyes.

Bider, clearly angry, turned and strode into the forest.

16

That night Runt awoke to find Bider standing over him. "Come with me," Bider said. It was an order.

Runt rose. "Where are we going?" he asked, even as he fell into step behind the white wolf.

"You'll see," Bider replied in his usual brusque way. Then he added, mysteriously, "You want a chance to make your father proud, don't you?"

A thrill ran along Runt's spine. *How will I do that?* he wanted to ask. *How will I ever do that?* But he knew better than to ply Bider with questions.

Raven appeared before them, balancing on the low bush just ahead.

"Guess what, Raven," Runt called. "I'm going to make my father proud."

"Be careful" was Raven's only response. And he stretched his wings and flew upward.

Runt watched Raven disappear beyond the thinning treetops, then turned his attention back to the white wolf. He didn't need Raven's warning. He knew all about being careful. Porcupine had taught him that lesson very thoroughly. But what, exactly, should he be careful of?

He followed Bider's silent steps through the forest. The night was still except for a light breeze rattling in the trees, the gentle swish of the fallen leaves underfoot.

When they arrived at a clearing Runt had never seen before, Bider squeezed through a wire fence and stopped abruptly. Runt crawled on his belly under the bottom wire and joined Bider.

"See," Bider said, and Runt did, indeed, see. The only problem was that he had no idea what he was seeing. The light from a half moon glinted off the splotchy hides of a herd of large black-and-white creatures. Larger than deer, not as big as moose. Succulent, even soft looking. They grazed the way moose and deer did, but Runt had never seen anything like them. Their smell was vaguely familiar, though.

"I've told King about them, but he won't listen," Bider said. "He refuses even to come with me to see."

"What are they?" Runt whispered. It was hard to believe they were real. Despite the fact that he and Bider were standing right out in the open, in full view, the creatures continued to crop grass as though they had never heard of wolves.

Even as Runt asked, he caught another scent. Not just the smell of living meat, but something more. The odor of the humans the creatures belonged to.

"They're called cows," Bider replied. "I thought you'd know all about them. Their owners are such good friends of yours."

"Friends?" Runt's legs had begun to tremble the moment he had distinguished the human scent, and he tried to steady himself. In the brief time he had been with the humans, he hadn't grown accustomed to the stink they left on everything. Now he had to struggle to keep from turning and running blindly back into the forest.

"I thought if you saw them, if you went back and told him, King would listen to you."

Runt was too astonished even to reply. Why would Bider think his father would listen to *him?*

One of the spotted black-and-white creatures was grazing close by, and she looked up, seeing them apparently for the first time. *Now,* Runt thought. *Now. She will understand her danger!*

But she didn't. She simply stood there and gazed in their direction, her dark eyes placid and incurious. Runt had never had such an odd encounter. When a wolf sees a moose or a deer, a kind of contract passes between them. The creature says, *Yes, you may take me* or *No, this isn't my time,* but always the prey understands. These cattle had no comprehension at all. Why, even foolish Rabbit knew better than to stand and stare into the eyes of a wolf!

If he had remained with the humans, let them care for him day after day, would he, too, have grown so stupid? The thought made Runt shudder.

"Let's get a talisman to take back to your

father," Bider said. "Maybe that will convince him." As he spoke, he loped lightly into the open grassy field, passing the cow who had been watching them and coming up behind another. This one went on grazing—didn't even take a few steps to move away—and when Bider got close, he jumped up and grabbed her dangling tail in his fierce jaws.

The cow's attention was caught, finally, with her tail. She bellowed, kicked, began to run. Already, though, Bider had fallen away. But he hadn't released his grip. He dropped to the ground with the cow's long, fringed tail sliced off neatly and clamped between his teeth.

The cow kept running, bellowing. Several others in the herd galloped a few clumsy steps to move out of the way of the running one's clamor. Then they went back to their grazing, as though a large white wolf in their midst, holding the severed tail of one of their own, was nothing to be particularly concerned about.

The wounded cow came up against another fence and stopped finally. She mooed pitifully, dripping blood from the stump where her tail used to be. Most of the rest of her kind still ignored her.

Bider turned and trotted across the pasture toward Runt, grinning, still holding the creature's tail in his teeth.

"Here," Bider said, dropping the tail at Runt's feet. "Take that home to your daddy. Let him see how sweet it is."

Runt sniffed the tail. It smelled rich and warm. It smelled, in fact, exactly like the meat he had been offered when he'd been with the humans, though he hadn't been ready to eat then. But there was no question it would be tasty. And a whole herd of these creatures— not one of which had the wits or strength to fight off a single wolf, let alone the pack— stood here before them.

His family was through being hungry. That was certain.

And Bider was going to let him present the gift of this easy food to his father!

Runt picked up the sweet-smelling tail in his teeth.

What will friend Raven have to say about this? he wondered. *What silly warning will he give*

*now? When the time comes, won't he be glad
enough to share a good meal?*

Provider, Runt decided as he trotted
beside Bider, the tail clamped tightly in his
teeth. That would be a good name. It had a
much better ring than Runt.

17

"No!" King didn't even bother to look at the gift Runt had dropped at his feet. He said it again. "No."

Runt was too stunned to speak, but he didn't need to. Bider spoke for him.

"Just take a taste," he whined. "These creatures aren't far away. And they're so stupid, they don't even know enough to run . . . or to fight, either. They just stand there waiting to be eaten. You've never seen anything like it."

With a nudge of his nose, Runt pushed the richly scented tail closer to his father.

King ignored Bider and spoke directly to Runt. "Haven't you learned yet? This meat isn't for us. It's been touched by *them*." And with that he walked away.

Touched by them. The phrase sent a chill through Runt's heart. If being touched by humans could ruin perfectly good meat, what had it done to him?

Runt turned helplessly back to Bider. Surely, he would explain that the meat was good, tell King again how easy the beasts were to kill. But the white wolf, clearly disgusted, had walked away, too.

Runt picked up the tail again and stood holding it. He shook his head to swing it back and forth. He could see the other pups watching him, but no one took his invitation to play.

Runt carried his prize off to his private place beneath the maple and gnawed it down to a collection of small bright bones.

18

When the sun settled below the tips of the trees, King rose and stretched. "It's time," he called to his pack. "Come."

"Past time, if you ask me," Bider muttered, but, as usual, King chose to ignore him.

Runt lifted his head, watching.

"Come," King said again, and this time his sweeping gaze took in all four pups. Apparently, they were to be a regular part of the hunters now.

Once more Runt remained silent through the howl, but he took up his accustomed place in the rear when the pack set off in their usual single file.

The wolves trotted at a steady pace for a couple of miles before they flushed a doe and her fawn. The two crashed away through the underbrush, outrunning the wolves almost before the pack could begin the chase.

The pack would have had a better chance if they could have gotten the pair out into the open. Or onto a frozen lake if the weather had been colder. Runt had heard his father talk about chasing prey onto the lakes in the winter, because the ice put animals with hard hooves at a disadvantage. This day, though, with the ice not yet formed, with the fawns grown strong and confident in their stride and everyone well fed at the end of a lush summer, the wolves could gain no advantage.

Farther on, King sniffed out a fresh trail and turned to follow it, but when they arrived at the small clearing where a moose was grazing, the huge animal, a cow in her prime, stared back at them with stubborn unconcern. Even Bider didn't argue that they should hurl themselves at an animal who refused to run, so they moved on.

They came upon a raspberry patch and paused to sample and then to feast, but a black bear arrived, an enormous, cross male intent on the same berries, and they moved on.

"Some confrontations," King said quietly, "aren't worth the cost."

Again, not even Bider disagreed.

They moved through the night this way, sometimes testing an animal into a brief dash, then, when their prospective prey proved strong, dropping back to preserve their own strength. Occasionally, they chose to move on because the animal they found was large and could hold them at bay. Sometimes they simply encountered no game. When they came upon the territorial marking left by the leader of a neighboring pack, King marked the edge of their own territory. Then they began to circle back.

Finally, as the rising sun filtered through the trees, King led them again toward their own clearing, their bellies still empty. Silver's limp had grown worse. Hunter, with her sore chest, was moving slowly, too. And the pups were so tired that they had begun to waver on their feet. But no one uttered any complaint, either about pain or fatigue or lack of food. This was the life of a wolf. Sometimes food was plentiful. Sometimes it was not. They all knew that.

When they reached their own clearing, each dropped to the ground and tumbled into nearly instant sleep.

It was later that Runt woke to see Bider standing at the far edge of the clearing, staring in the direction of the sleeping King. After a long moment, the white wolf turned and slipped away, disappearing among the trees. Runt didn't call after him to ask where he was going.

He didn't have to ask. He knew. His stomach rumbled at the thought.

19

The next time Runt awakened, Bider was emerging from the forest, his belly distended, his face bloodied by the feast he had just finished. He swaggered up to King, who was just waking, too, and stood in front of him. With King's eyes full on him, he regurgitated a steaming pile of meat, dropping it before his leader as though he were feeding a pup.

"For you," Bider said. "I thought you might be hungry."

Runt held his breath. Such deep insult was mixed with the gift that he could not even guess at his father's response.

King said nothing. He looked neither at Bider nor at the meat the white wolf had brought back in his belly. He merely rose, stretched, gave out an enormous yawn, and walked away.

The newly awakened pups rose, too, and began to edge toward the feast.

"Leave it!" their father growled.

Even before his nose had confirmed what he knew, Runt understood why King had refused the gift. This meat came from one of the cows that belonged to the humans.

Bider remained standing there, next to his gift. His yellow eyes studied each of them in turn, daring them to come for the food, despite King's command. No one did. However hungry they might be, no one was ready to disobey their leader.

Runt didn't dare disobey, either, but he stood several feet from the steaming offering and watched both Bider and his father closely.

What was wrong with King? Was he so afraid of humans that he was afraid even of the placid, stupid beasts who supplied this marvelous food?

Runt shivered. What was wrong with *him*? He was questioning his own father.

And yet the question remained.

When no one moved toward the meat, the white wolf gulped it again. Runt watched him eat, his own mouth watering.

Then, just as everyone was turning away, relieved that the near confrontation had passed, King turned back to give Bider a stern stare. But this time, instead of lowering his head and tucking his tail as he had always done before, the white wolf lifted his chin, pricked his ears, raised his hackles. A direct challenge such as that could not be ignored.

The fight that followed was silent and terrible. For months the pack had been accustomed to Bider's constant encroachments on King's rule. A rude word, eyes too direct, ears cocked at the wrong angle, tail too high. But King had always handled the threat to the pack's order easily, with a growl, a stare, a loud chomping of the teeth. And Bider would return to his place again, submissive, properly respectful.

But this time the white wolf came at King with his tail high, his hackles raised, his gaze unwavering. He said nothing, just came straight on, clearly having made up his mind to bide his time no longer.

The rest of the pack barely breathed. Runt edged closer, but he knew better—as everyone did—than to interfere in any way with the fight.

Bider threw himself at King, his mouth open, his teeth gleaming. After a too-brief struggle, King was down and Bider was on top, snapping and snarling, snatching at King's shoulder with vicious teeth.

Stop! Runt wanted to cry, but he didn't. No one else cried out, either.

Then, with a mighty effort, King twisted, threw Bider off, scrambled to his feet again. The two wolves circled once more. Blood dripped from the jagged tear in King's shoulder.

"Father!" Sniffer cried, but a look from Silver warned her, and she said no more.

Bider feinted, withdrew. King lunged, snapped, came away with white fur clinging to his lips. The two threw themselves at each other, gnashing their teeth, rolling on the ground, locked together until the black fur and the white fur seemed like separate parts of the same being.

Then, as quickly as it had begun, the fight was over. King stood over Bider, his teeth clamped on the white wolf's throat. The black wolf panted and bled, but he was victorious.

Bider lay on the ground, limp, waiting.

The others waited, too.

Now, Runt thought. *Now. My father will kill him.* And though he wanted to cry out, Don't! Runt held his breath, held his entire self in silent suspension.

If Bider had been the winner, King might never have risen again. Compassion was not in the white wolf's nature. But King was the one on top, and he had always ruled with a gentle authority. He stood for a long time, staring down at his would-be usurper, then took a quiet step back, allowing Bider to find his feet once more. Both wolves bled profusely.

"Go!" King said.

And Bider did. Slinking off across the clearing, across the stream, his head low, his tail tight against his belly, he disappeared into the deep woods without once looking back.

The pack would feel Bider's absence. Food would be harder to come by without the white wolf's prowess. Their days would be quieter, too, less filled with tension. They all settled to the ground slowly, one at a time, and sighed.

Only Runt continued to watch the dark

place between the trees into which Bider had disappeared.

Bider knew how to get food. Easily and in quantity. Food that his father refused. Bider had shown him where and how.

Should a pup named Runt follow?

20

The night was long beyond imagining. King made himself a bed at one edge of the clearing, and all the pack circled him, licking his wounds, murmuring reassurance and respect. All except Bider, of course, whose absence no one mentioned.

Runt tried once to approach his father, to reach him to nudge his chin in the way a young son should. But Leader pushed past him, and the black pup withdrew, returning to his accustomed place beneath the maple. He lay there, his chin resting on his paws, watching.

Lying in the dark, though, he could not rid himself of the memory of Bider, bloody and defeated, slinking away into the forest. The white wolf was being tended by no one.

Would he, Runt, be a bider one day, too?

Would there ever be a true place for him in this or any pack?

Morning had come before King's bleeding finally stopped. When the sky had gone from pewter to a pale rose, the black wolf gathered strength to rise stiffly and move off to the stream for a drink of water. The pack let out a collective sigh. Their leader would survive. If King survived, they would continue to be who they were meant to be, a family, each single wolf grown stronger for its connection with the others.

With King wounded and Bider gone, with Silver and Hunter both still injured and the pups too young yet to be much help on a hunt, the pack faced certain hunger. They had survived hunger before, of course. Wolves are often required to survive hunger. But this time winter was coming on, and the pack was badly depleted. This hunger was going to be serious.

Runt lay at the edge of the clearing, gazing at his family, loving them all. His gentle mother, Hunter, Leader, Runner, Sniffer. King, so proud, usually so strong. But even looking at them, one after the other, he couldn't stop thinking of Bider and of the meat that waited so close at hand. Meat that would bring back his father's strength. The pack's strength.

Except that King would never accept it.

That great beast Bider had brought down was feeding the white wolf, restoring him, perhaps even encouraging him to return to battle. The meat would feed other creatures of the forest, too. Even Raven. But not King or his family.

Runt knew his father was wrong. It was possible for his father to be wrong! Humans were good, kind. Runt knew this for a fact. The meat of their beasts was good, too. And easy to get. Very easy.

But if his father wouldn't listen to him—and what father, after all, would listen to a pup he had named Runt?—then there was no way to save him. Or anyone else in his family.

All that was left for Runt to do was to save himself.

21

Runt paused once, just at the edge of the close-growing trees, listening to see if someone from the pack might call him back. No one did.

He moved out, taking the direction Bider had earlier.

He found the place again easily, following his nose, following his memory of humps of rock and fallen trees, even of patches of flowers. In the open pasture beyond the easily penetrated fence, the beasts owned by humans grazed. They moved slowly as through a dream of thin morning light. At the edge of the pasture lay the carcass of the one Bider had killed. The smell of meat filled the air, rich and compelling.

And as Runt had guessed, Bider was there before him, feasting again. When Runt approached, the white wolf growled, deep in his throat. "What are you doing here?"

"I came to see if you were all right," Runt replied.

"Of course I'm all right. Why wouldn't I be?" Bider tore off a hunk of meat from the carcass and swallowed it in a great gulp.

Drool dripped from Runt's tongue at the sight, but he kept a respectful distance. He had seen what Bider's teeth could do. Looking at Bider, he could see what King's teeth had done, too. The white wolf was bleeding from a wound on his back, and one leg was deeply slashed.

Still . . . Runt was hungry. "May I?" He took a step toward the food.

"Why should I share my kill with the likes of you?" Bider growled again. "You'll only go back to *him* when your belly's full."

Would he? "No," Runt said. "Never."

Bider made no reply, just tore off another hunk of meat and gulped it down. Runt was almost certain he was smiling, though. Whether with something like affection or merely satisfaction at seeing the pack break up he couldn't tell.

"I could help you hunt," Runt offered.

"Help me hunt? Do you think I need help from—"

Runt knew what Bider was going to say. "Do you think I need help from a runt like you?" But the white wolf left the sentence unfinished. In fact, he stopped eating entirely and suddenly sat back, perfectly still, his head twisted at an odd angle. He looked surprised, though Runt couldn't tell why.

Runt took a few steps closer. Maybe Bider had eaten his fill and was ready now to share.

"No! Don't! You mustn't!" a hoarse voice shouted.

Runt glanced over to see Raven perched on the fence. What was that annoying bird doing here now? And what was he worried about, anyway? That two wolves feasting on this huge carcass wouldn't leave enough scraps for one bird? Runt decided to ignore him.

"I know I'm not very big," he said to Bider. "And I know l have a lot to learn. But I will grow bigger, and you can teach me." He licked one of the cow's hind hooves. It had been too long since he had eaten.

"No!" Raven screamed again. And this

time he landed directly in front of Runt.

The black pup stepped back, away from the bird, but he was rigid with impatience. "Why shouldn't I eat," he demanded to know, "if Bider is willing to share?"

"Can't you see? This meat has been touched by *them!*"

There it was again. Such ignorance. Humans contaminate all they touch. Well, Runt knew better. He stepped around Raven.

But before he could take his first mouthful, Bider gave a sudden jerk. He lifted his front paws to his face, pulling at his muzzle. His eyes, still on Runt, looked bewildered.

Raven flapped his wings and rose into the air only to drop again to the ground at Runt's side. "Look around you!" he screamed. "Just look! Can't you see?"

For the first time since he had arrived at the pasture, Runt looked. Not only was Bider behaving strangely, trying to vomit now but unable to bring anything up, but other animals lay on the ground. A jay. A wolverine. A score of mice and velvet shrews. Even a bald eagle lay still and dead, just a few feet from the meat he had been eating.

"Poison!" Raven croaked. "The humans have poisoned the meat."

Even as Raven spoke, Bider struggled to his feet. He stumbled toward Raven as though attacking him would change the truth of what had been said. But before he could reach the black bird, his front legs gave out, he lurched forward, and his jaw struck the ground. Saliva bubbled from his lips.

Runt went still, the sweet-smelling meat just inches from his nose. He stared at the white wolf and at the rest of the animals lying on the ground, dead before the feast.

Runt had seen death before, of course, but never in so terrible a way as this.

Bider struggled to rise, fell forward, did not get up again. His yellow eyes remained open. Haunted.

And that was when the sun broke free of the trees and shone down on the carnage below. Runt looked at the white wolf, utterly still, his face contorted in pain. He looked at the other poor poisoned creatures. Then he looked beyond them all to the brilliant day.

He sat back on his haunches, trembling. "I—I," he said to Raven, "I thank you."

Raven bowed his head modestly, drew a horny claw through his beak.

Runt looked for a long time at the dead animals scattered in the dewy grass. "Is it true?" he asked at last. "Do humans really contaminate all they touch?"

"Not all," Raven replied. "But enough."

Runt thought about that. "Tell me," he asked finally, "what should I do? Where should I go?"

"Home," Raven replied. "Your father is waiting for you. Go home."

Runt shook his head. "My father *named* me," he said. There seemed to be nothing more to say.

"Your father loves you. Perhaps more than all the rest."

"*Puh!*" Runt let out an explosion of disbelieving breath.

"King watches you." Raven spoke gently. "He worries about you. He wants desperately for you to survive. If that's not love, I don't know what is."

But Runt could only shake his head again.

22

After Raven flew away, Runt sat for a long time, surrounded by the carnage. When several crows, a skunk, and a young badger showed up to feed, he warned them of the poison. Badger, apparently certain that Runt was trying to keep the entire feast to himself, moved off only as far as the underbrush on the other side of the fence and squatted there belligerently, waiting for the wolf pup to go away.

Runt did finally, leaving stubborn Badger to his fate. He lowered his head and plodded away without taking note of the direction he chose. Since he had no place to go, the direction hardly mattered.

He couldn't return to his family bearing no gift except news of Bider's death. And that was hardly a gift. Letting them know that he himself had faced death and survived, as Raven said his father had always hoped, wasn't enough of a gift, either. Merely surviving gave nothing to his family.

He could, of course, go back and tell his father, "You were right. Humans mean death." But somehow that didn't seem to be the point. Not the whole one, anyway. It remained equally true that humans had helped him and that they would have helped Thinker, too, if he had stumbled upon them as Runt had. Perhaps the truth was that humans were a mixture, aggressive and kind, greedy and generous. Like wolves.

Runt wove his way beneath the birch trees, their leaves as gold as a wolf's eyes. He pushed through a stand of pine, heavy with cones. He plodded, without paying particular attention to what lay before him, into a small bower created by overhanging limbs. And there he found the moose.

It was the old bull his family and Bider had pursued, the one they had wounded.

The colossal animal lunged to his feet and stood before Runt, swaying like a tree in a strong wind.

Take me, the beast's eyes said. *My time has come. You may take me.*

Runt's heart pounded; his breath came in ragged bursts. Was he really brave enough to take this huge animal and bring the good meat home to his family? It was as though this moose were the gift he had been waiting for, for so long. And here the old bull stood, practically giving himself to Runt.

The wolf pup began to dance, first to one side, then to the other. But if the moose was ready to die, he clearly wasn't going to do it without a fight. Whichever side Runt chose, the bull lowered his head and swung his enormous antlers in Runt's direction. The antlers were at least six feet across, and after a few futile attempts to get close, Runt backed away.

He considered leaping up and grabbing the beast's nostrils, the way Helper had done, but he remembered what had come of Helper's grabbing on there. And he remembered, too, what it felt like to fly off the fellow's hind leg.

There seemed to be no way . . . unless size could be an advantage. Not being big, but being small. Small and young and quick.

The beast snorted and pawed the ground.

Moose were notorious for their bad eye-sight. And this fellow had clearly lost blood from the wounds left by his first encounter with the pack. He was growing weak and wouldn't be able to do anything very quickly. So if a small pup moved in fast and low to the ground, then leapt for his throat—

Wouldn't King be— What would he be? Disappointed once more, probably. Disappointed that his son had no more sense than to try to take on this mammoth creature by himself. Disappointed that Runt didn't understand that the main strength of a pack was that they worked together in all they did.

The old moose stood there, teetering on his long legs, and peered muzzily in Runt's direction. Clearly, he was waiting to see what the wolf pup was going to do.

And that was when Runt decided. For weeks now he had been keeping his voice still, but he had a voice, a voice and a story to tell. About Bider. About the poisoned meat. His family must know about the poisoned meat. And about the bull moose, about the moose waiting to die, waiting to give strength to his family. His family must know about all of it.

And so the small black pup lifted his face to the soft blue sky and howled, loud and clear. "Come," he sang. "You must come. I have found Moose."

His voice rose and rose on the sunlit air, then slid back down and rose again. He sang until an answer came floating back through the crisp fall day.

"Moose?" It was King. "Who calls my family to feast?"

"It is I," the pup answered, and he was going to add his name, Runt, but he couldn't make himself say it. So he said again only, "It is I. The one who wears your black fur and white star."

At first, Runt heard no response. Only silence followed his father's question, his answer. And then the song came again, eerie and beautiful, ringing through the forest.

"My son," his mother howled in her high and tender voice.

"Brother!" sang Hunter and the pups.

And then his father's voice boomed out again, more powerful than all the rest despite the wounds he had just endured in battle.

"Singer. My son Singer," he howled. "Wait for us there. We come."

So . . . he was no longer Runt. His father had given him a new name. At last. The small black pup turned the name over and over to test the feel of it.

Singer. He would be Singer. And surely he did have a song to sing, a unique and sad and beautiful song, given especially to him.

He could sing about death. He could sing about longing. He could sing about loving. About loving his family and the sweet world that gave them all life.

He could sing about an aging and injured moose, awaiting his fate.

Singer lifted his face again to the pale morning sky and howled once more. "Come, my dear ones!" he sang. "Come. The feast waits."

Afterword

Wolves are complex and varied creatures. Human response to wolves has been complex and varied, too. For centuries white settlers on the North American continent called wolves evil, cowards, murderers. They brought this attitude with them from Europe where both rabies and dog-wolf interbreeding sometimes made wolves dangerous to humans. The fear created by such encounters still colors many of the stories we tell very young children, stories such as "Little Red Riding Hood" and "The Three Little Pigs."

Native populations on this continent, mostly hunters themselves, had a much different attitude toward wolves. They admired them for their family spirit and their hunting skill, for their power and intelligence and the close relationship they had with their world. Unfortunately, the attitudes of the Europeans prevailed, and from the seventeenth through the twentieth centuries wolves were almost eradicated in North America. They were killed for money, for sport, for vengeance. They were shot from airplanes and caught in traps and poisoned, taking other equally innocent creatures with them into death. It was only in the late twentieth century that we began to question the assumptions that justified this slaughter.

Runt and his pack are, of course, entirely fictional. And yet most of what they do in this story—except for talking—is based on observations made by wolf biologists studying these fascinating creatures. Wolves have been observed rejoicing over the birth of their young, burying dead pups, playing jokes on one another and on the creatures around them, baby-sitting, interacting with ravens, nurturing and disciplining and teaching their young, caring for the elderly and the ill, marking their territory, jockeying for power, and bobtailing cows.

And they do, occasionally, slay animals such as cows that humans prefer to reserve for their own killing. In northern Minnesota, where wolves have made enough of a comeback for their status to be reduced from endangered to threatened, it is understandable that some farmers object strenuously to their presence. Occasionally, someone attempts to eradicate the animal by illegally poisoning the carcasses of wolf-killed cattle. One of the ironic results of this poisoning has been to teach those packs inclined to do their hunting from human-owned herds to make new kills each time. However, biologists who have studied the situation say that in Minnesota only one wolf in ninety ever actually chooses domestic livestock for its prey.

There is much we still don't understand about wolves, and what we do understand changes each year. But we know that a pack is usually made up of a single breeding pair and their offspring, especially the young ones who are still dependent and the yearlings not yet ready to go off on their own. We know that other adults can be adopted into a pack, that bider wolves exist, constantly challenging the lead, or alpha, male or female for power. We know that no wolf is exactly the same as any other wolf, that they are as different from one another as you and I.

While wolves don't use words to think and speak, they communicate, in ways that are probably far more complex than we yet understand, using body posture, facial ex-

pressions, and vocalization. One biologist
even maintains that wolves will not step on
flowers and that, prior to their making a kill,
an understanding passes between them and
their wild prey, a kind of death contract. In
any case, these animals are fascinating and
intelligent, and if we allow them to continue
to live among us, we will be learning from
and about them for many years to come.

Wolves are exclusive creatures. I have
never seen one in the wild. Few people have.
But I have heard them howl, I have seen their
droppings and the remains of their kills, and I
have felt the thrill of knowing that, however
tenuously, they still inhabit this world I live
in. If this story increases the reader's empathy
for the wolf, I will be glad. If it helps bolster
our willingness to protect the wilderness
wolves must have to survive, it will have
served its subject well.

Bibliography

Written for, or of special interest to, young readers

FICTION

George, Jean Craighead. *Julie*. Illustrated by Wendell Minor. New York: HarperCollins, 1994.

———. *Julie of the Wolves*. Illustrated by John Schoenherr. New York: Harper & Row, 1972.

———. *Julie's Wolf Pack*. Illustrated by Wendell Minor. New York: HarperCollins, 1997.

———. *Look to the North: A Wolf Pup Diary*. Illustrated by Lucia Washburn. New York: HarperCollins, 1997.

———. *The Moon of the Grey Wolves*. Illustrated by Sal Catalano. New York: HarperCollins, 1991.

Murphy, Jim. *Call of the Wolves*. Illustrated by Mark Alan Weatherby. New York: Scholastic, 1989.

NONFICTION

Johnson, Sylvia A., and Alic Aamodt. *Wolf Pack: Tracking Wolves in the Wild*. Minneapolis: Lerner Publications, 1985.

The Language and Music of the Wolves, including "The Wolf You Never Knew," narrated by Robert Redford, an audio tape.

Swinburne, Stephen R. *Once a Wolf: How Biologists Fought to Bring Back the Grey Wolf*. Photographs by Jim Brandenburg. Boston: Houghton Mifflin, 1999.

Written for adults

Bomford, Liz. *The Complete Wolf*. New York: St. Martin's, 1993.

Busch, Robert H. *The Wolf Almanac*. New York: Lyons, 1995.

Caras, Roger. *The Custer Wolf: Biography of an American Renegade*. Illustrated by Charles Frace. Boston: Little, Brown, 1966.

Grooms, Steve. *The Return of the Wolf*. Minocqua, Wis.: NorthWord, 1993.

Lawrence, R. D. *In Praise of Wolves*. New York: Holt, 1986.

Lopez, Barry H. *Of Wolves and Men*. Photographs by John Baugness. New York: Scribner's, 1978.

Mech, L. David. *The Wolf: The Ecology and Behavior of an Endangered Species*. Minneapolis: University of Minnesota Press, 1995.

————, ed. *The Wolves of Minnesota: Howl in the Heartland*. Stillwater, Minn.: Voyageur Press, 2000.

Steinhart, Peter. *The Company of Wolves*. New York: Knopf, 1995.

Turbak, Gary. *Twilight Hunters: Wolves, Coyotes, and Foxes*. Photographs by Alan Carey. Flagstaff, Ariz.: Northland, 1987.